The Super Adventures of OLLIE AND BEA

WISE-QUACKERS

Here's Ollie and his best friend, Bea.

Hi, Bea!

Hey, Ollie!
Sorry we're late.

Today, like every day for these friends, is a
MYSTERY-SOLVING DAY!

RENÉE TREML

PICTURE WINDOW BOOKS
a capstone imprint

Published by Picture Window Books, an imprint of Capstone.
1710 Roe Crest Drive, North Mankato, Minnesota 56003
capstonepub.com

Library of Congress Cataloging-in-Publication Data is available
on the Library of Congress website.
ISBN: 9781666314885 (hardcover)
ISBN: 9781666330984 (paperback)
ISBN: 9781666330991 (ebook PDF)

Summary: Everything is just duckie until Bea's stuffed animal gets stuck up in a
tree. Will Ollie admit his role in this *hoo*-dunnit and let Bea help him rescue the
treasured toy?

Designed by Kay Fraser

Printed and bound in the USA. 4608

TABLE OF CONTENTS

CHAPTER 1

FOWL PLAY

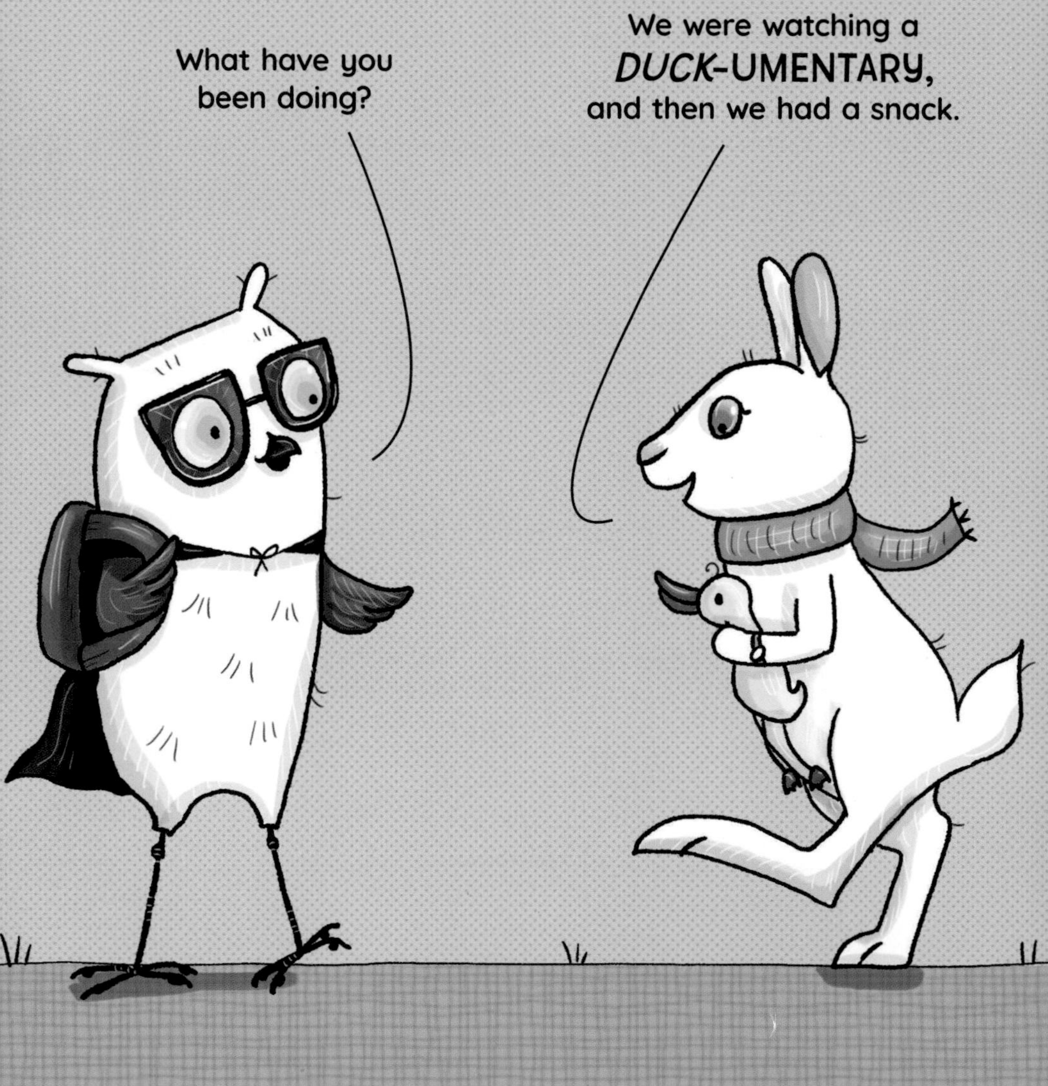
What have you been doing?
We were watching a *DUCK*-UMENTARY, and then we had a snack.

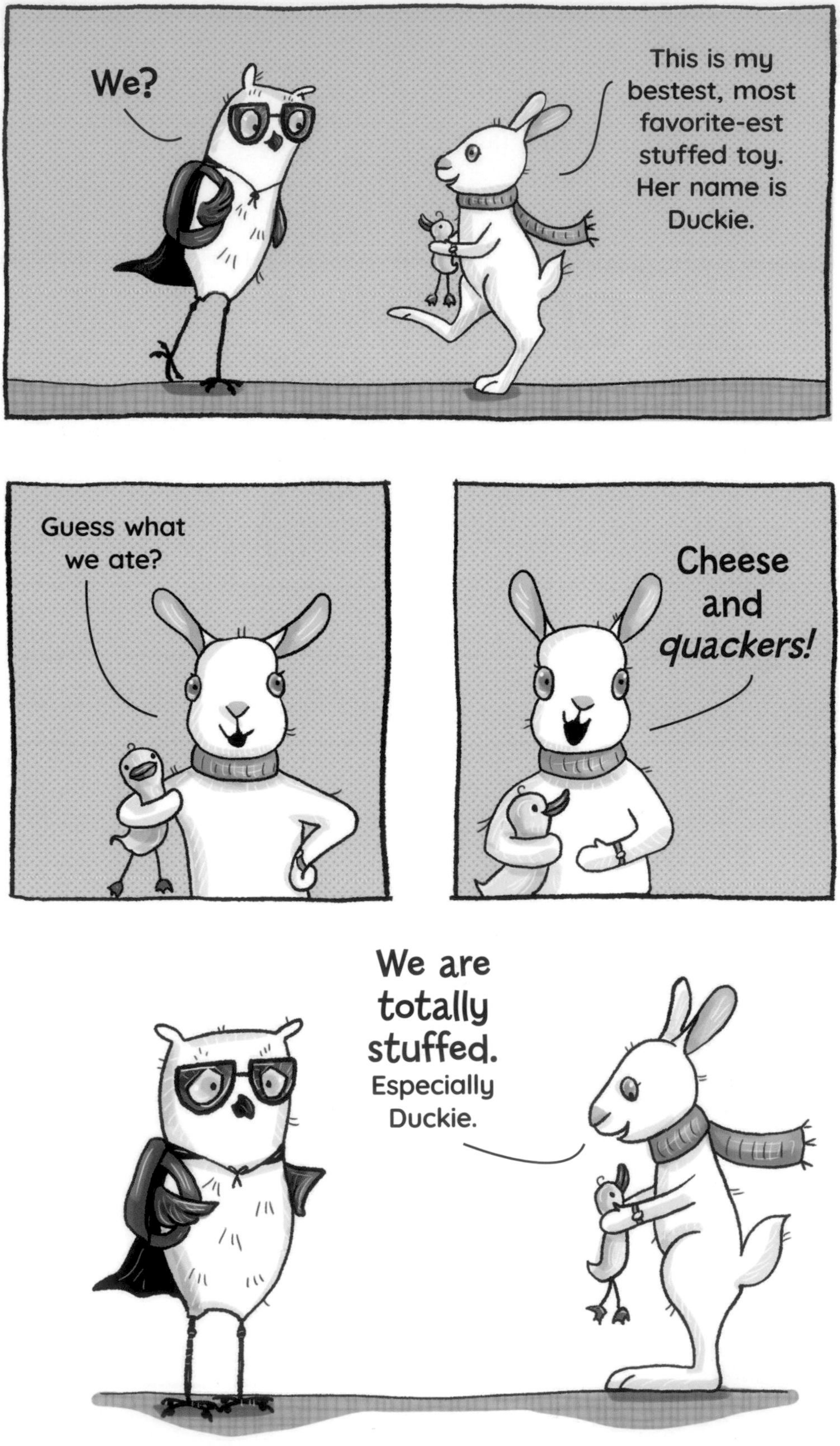
We?
This is my bestest, most favorite-est stuffed toy. Her name is Duckie.
Guess what we ate?
Cheese and *quackers!*
We are totally stuffed.
Especially Duckie.

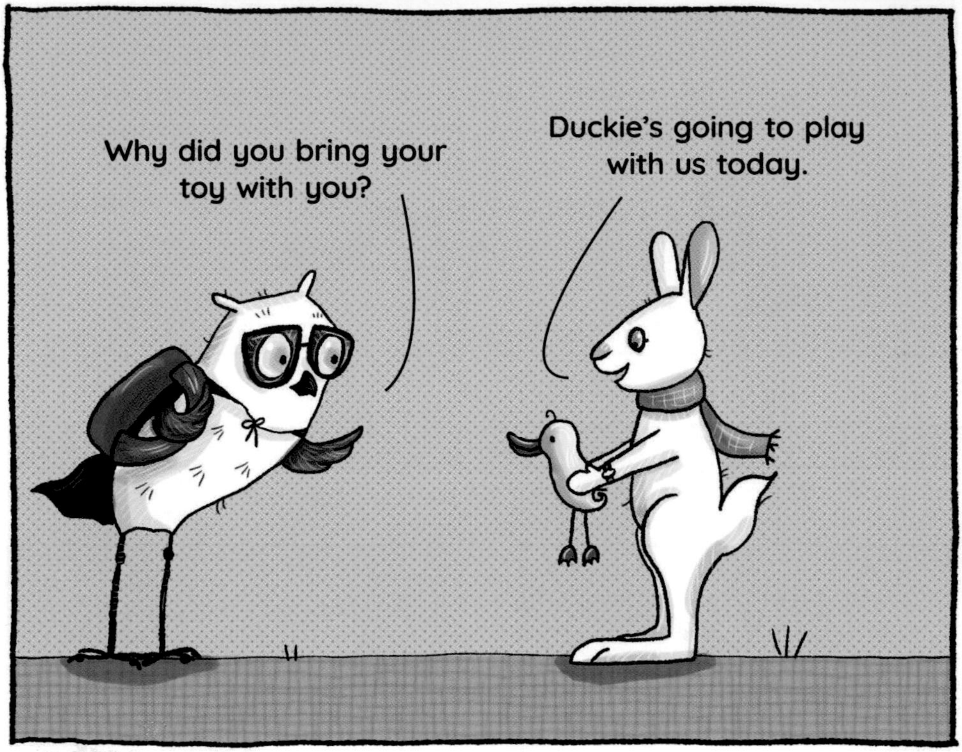
Why did you bring your toy with you?
Duckie's going to play with us today.

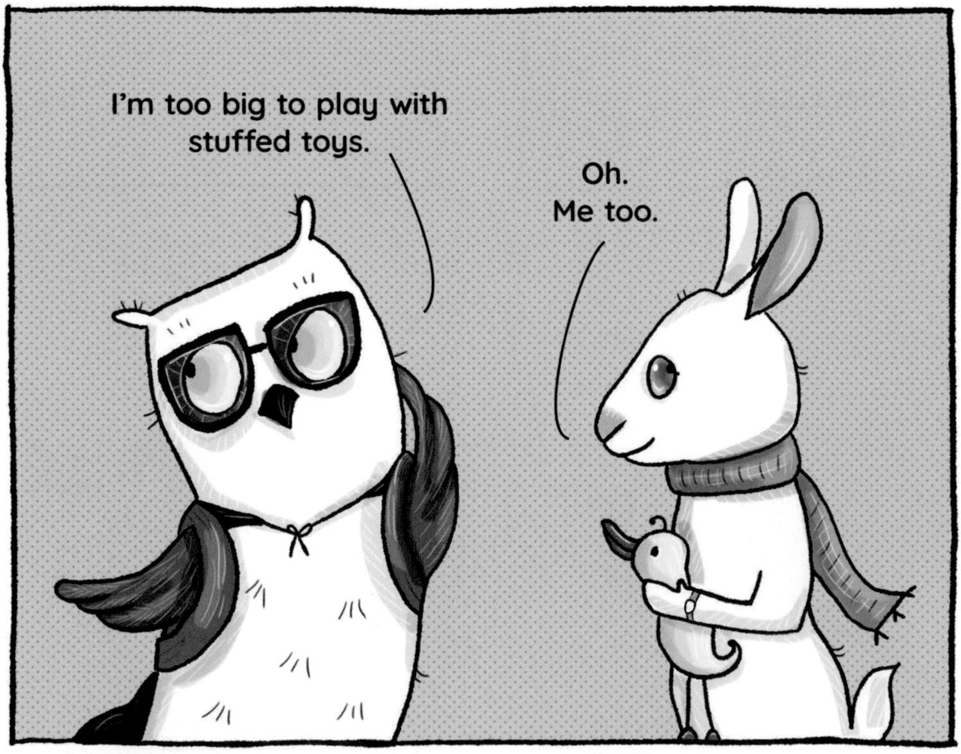
I'm too big to play with stuffed toys.
Oh.
Me too.

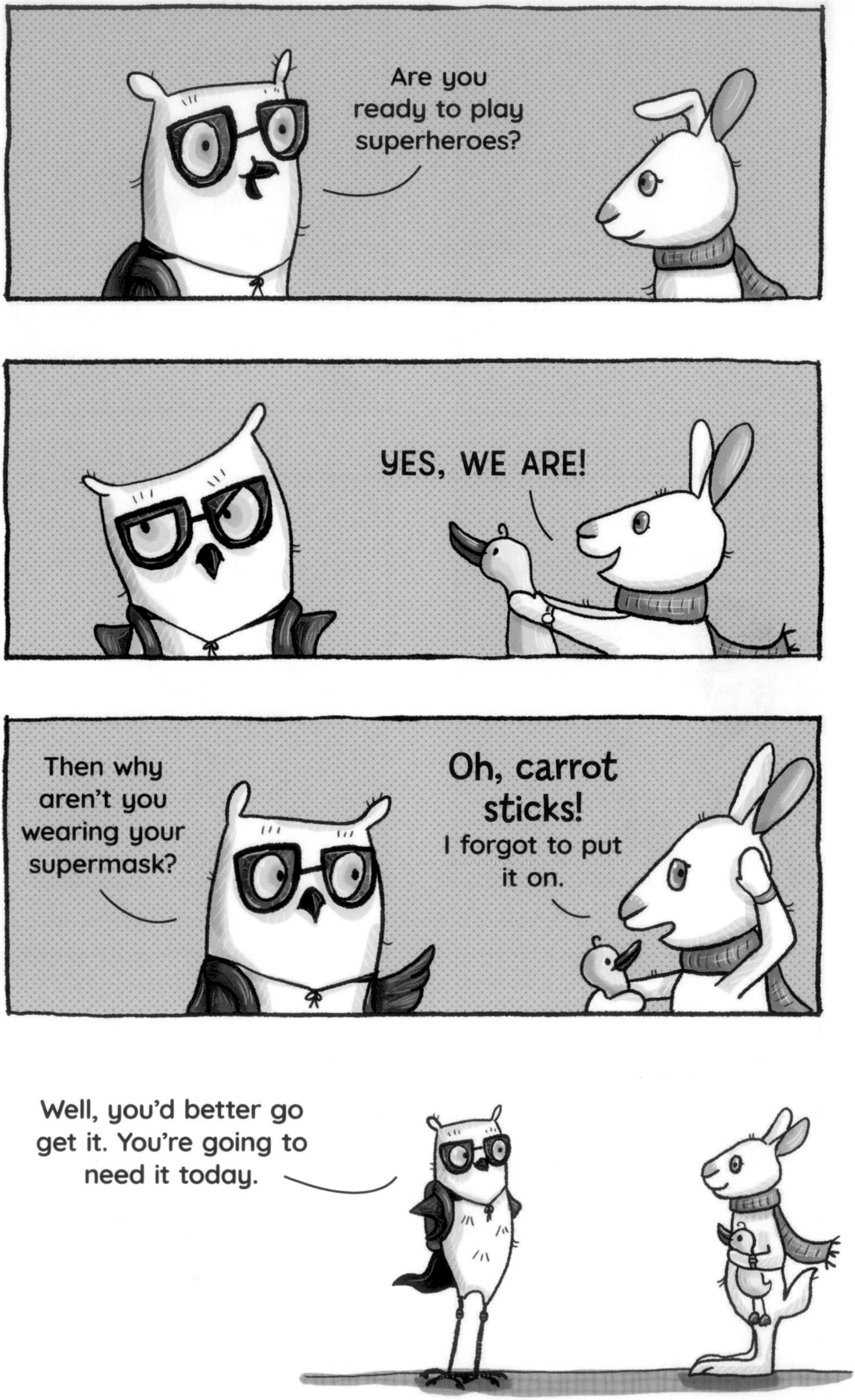
Are you ready to play superheroes?
YES, WE ARE!
Then why aren't you wearing your supermask?
Oh, carrot sticks! I forgot to put it on.
Well, you'd better go get it. You're going to need it today.

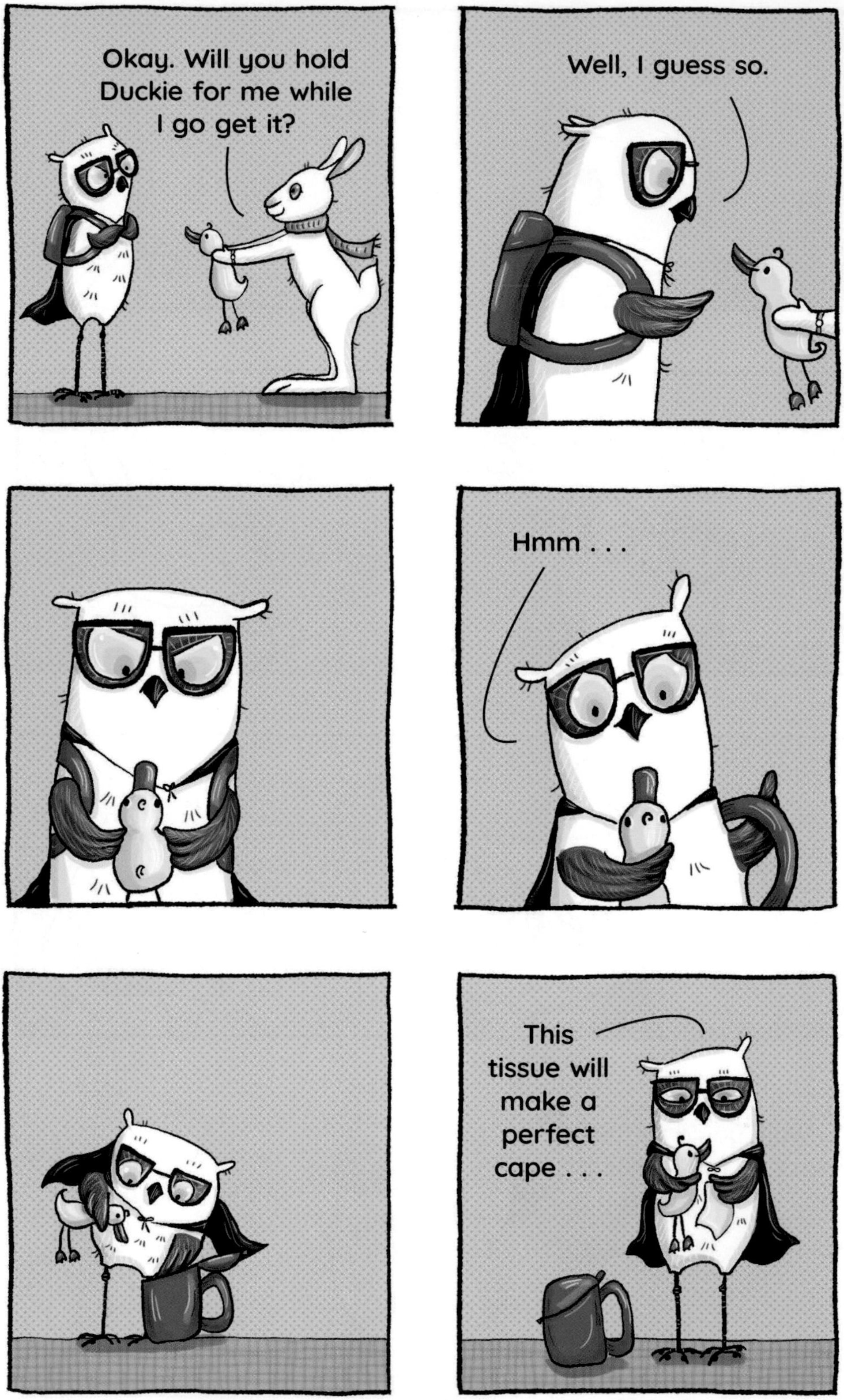
Okay. Will you hold Duckie for me while I go get it?
Well, I guess so.
Hmm . . .
This tissue will make a perfect cape . . .

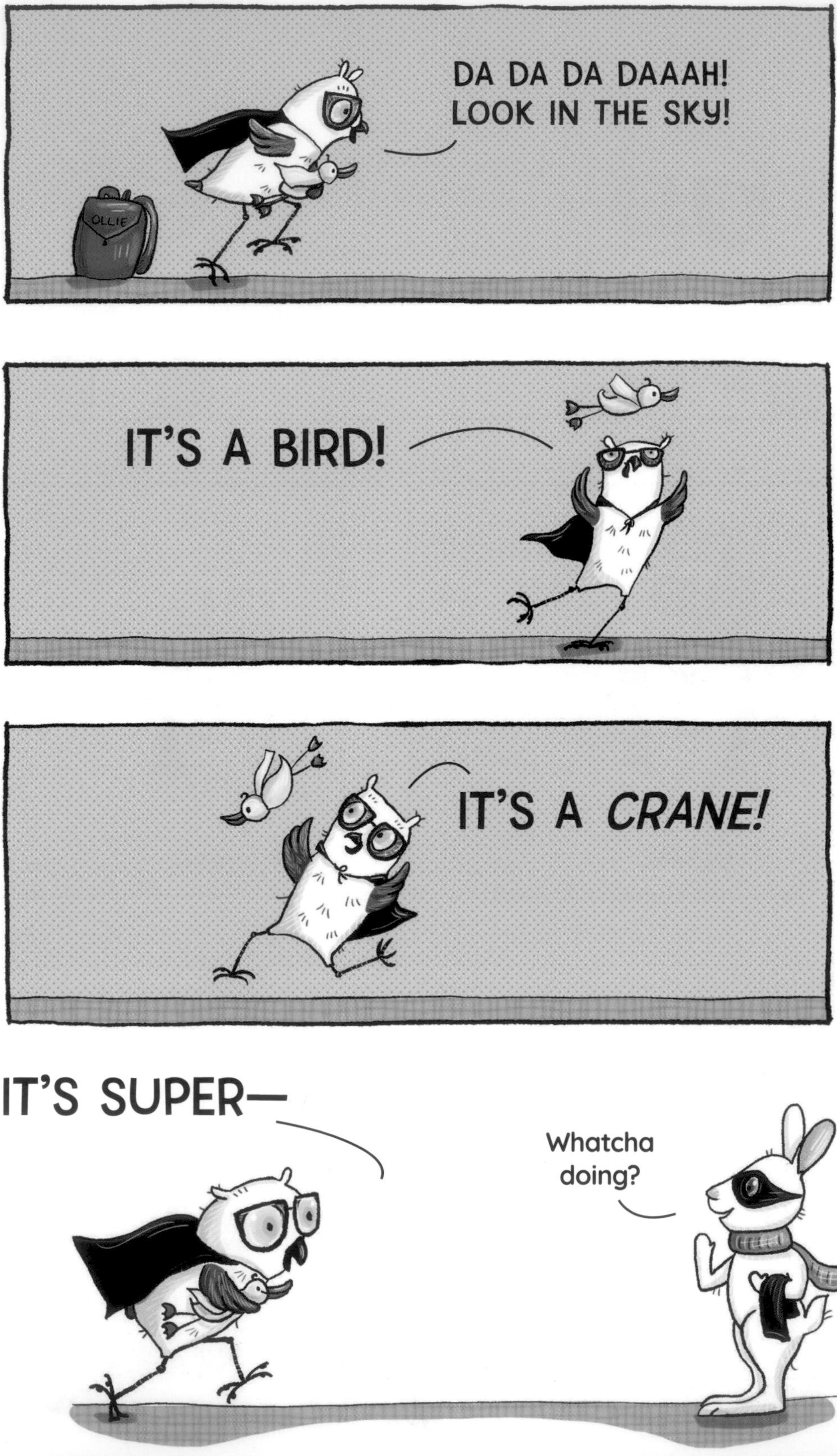
OLLIE
DA DA DA DAAAH! LOOK IN THE SKY!
IT'S A BIRD!
IT'S A *CRANE!*
IT'S SUPER—
Whatcha doing?

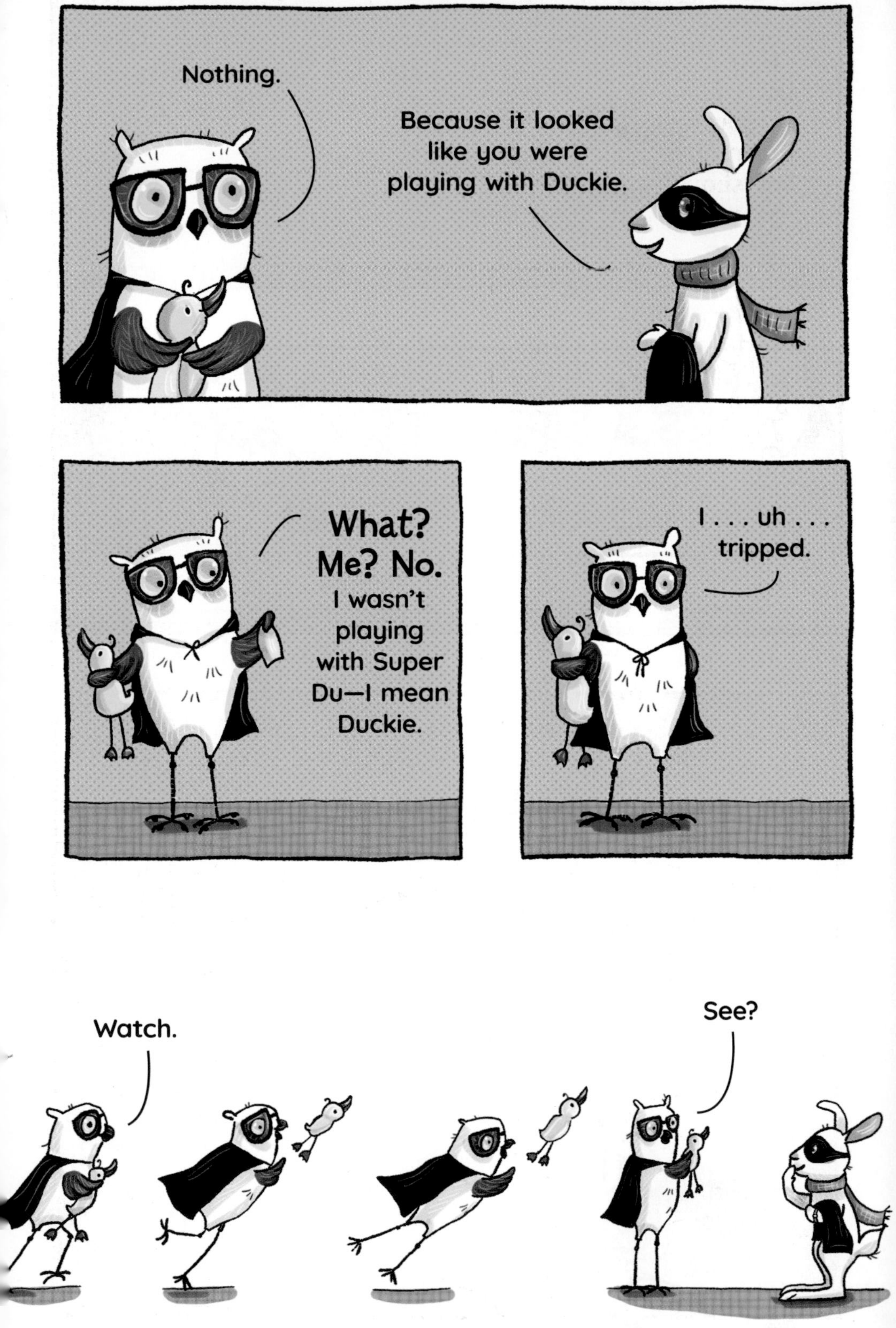
Nothing.
Because it looked like you were playing with Duckie.
What? Me? No. I wasn't playing with Super Du—I mean Duckie.
I . . . uh . . . tripped.
Watch.
See?

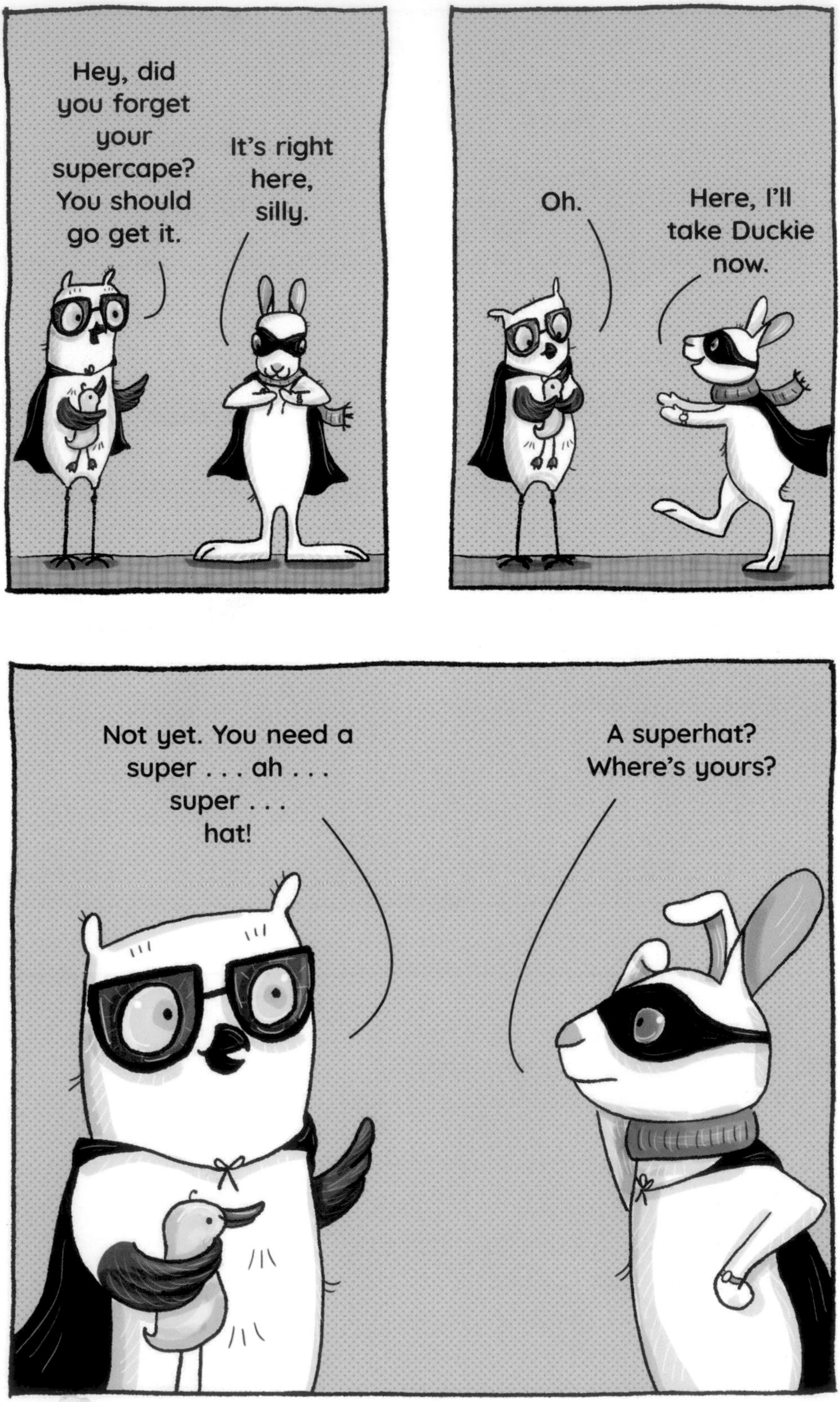
Hey, did you forget your supercape? You should go get it.
It's right here, silly.
Oh.
Here, I'll take Duckie now.
Not yet. You need a super . . . ah . . . super . . . hat!
A superhat? Where's yours?

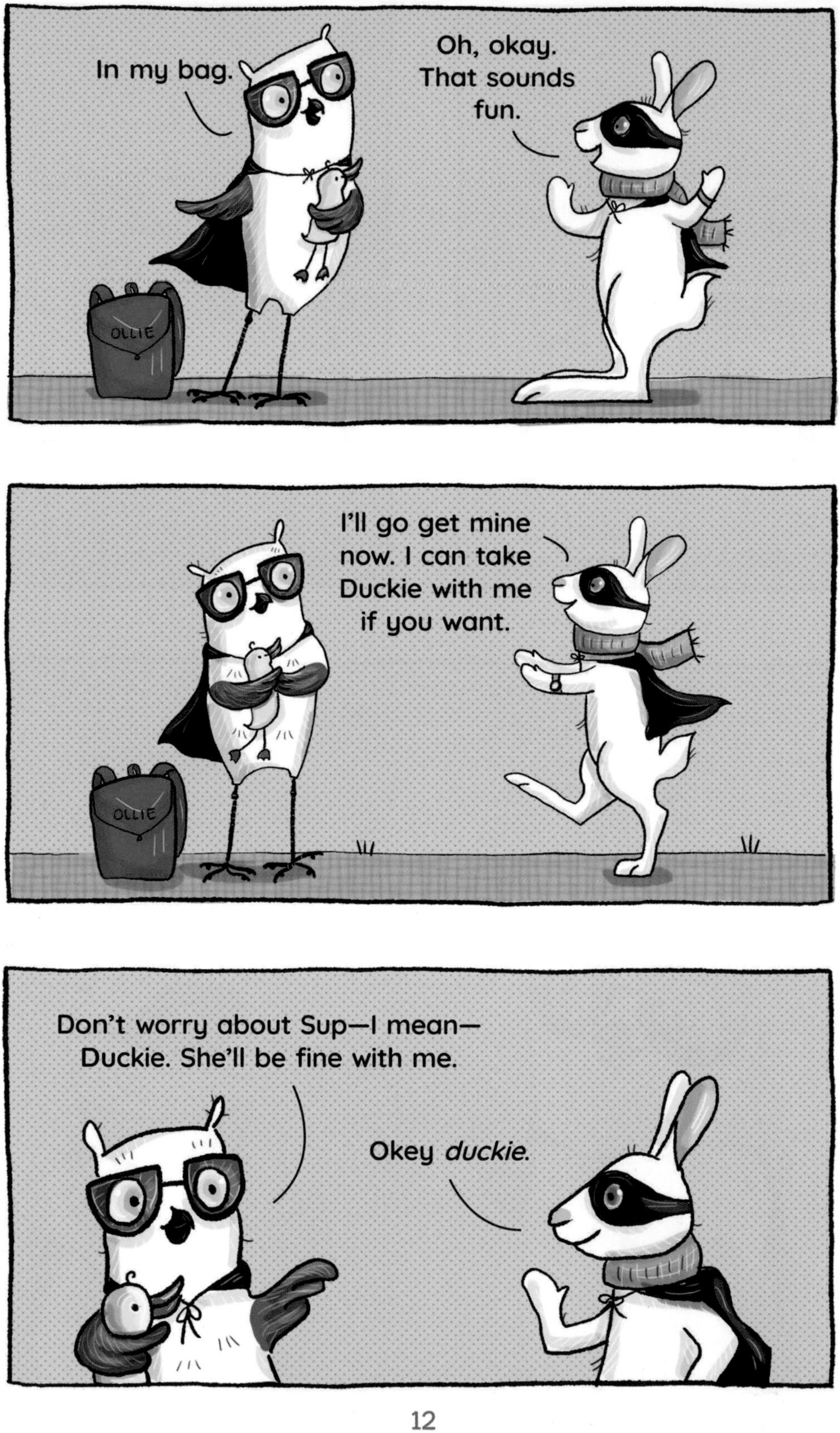
In my bag.
Oh, okay. That sounds fun.
OLLIE
I'll go get mine now. I can take Duckie with me if you want.
OLLIE
Don't worry about Sup—I mean—Duckie. She'll be fine with me.
Okey *duckie.*

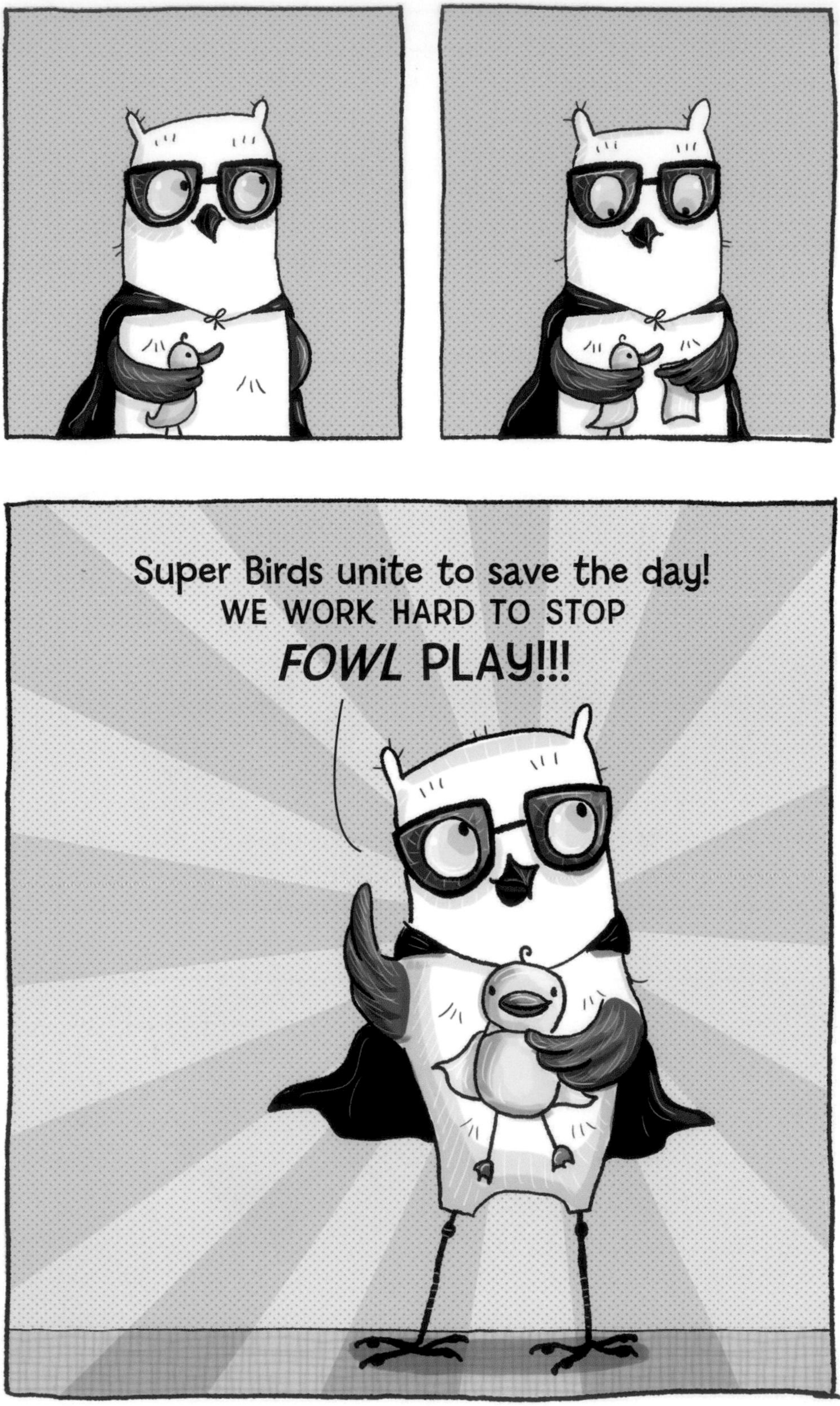
Super Birds unite to save the day!
WE WORK HARD TO STOP
FOWL PLAY!!!

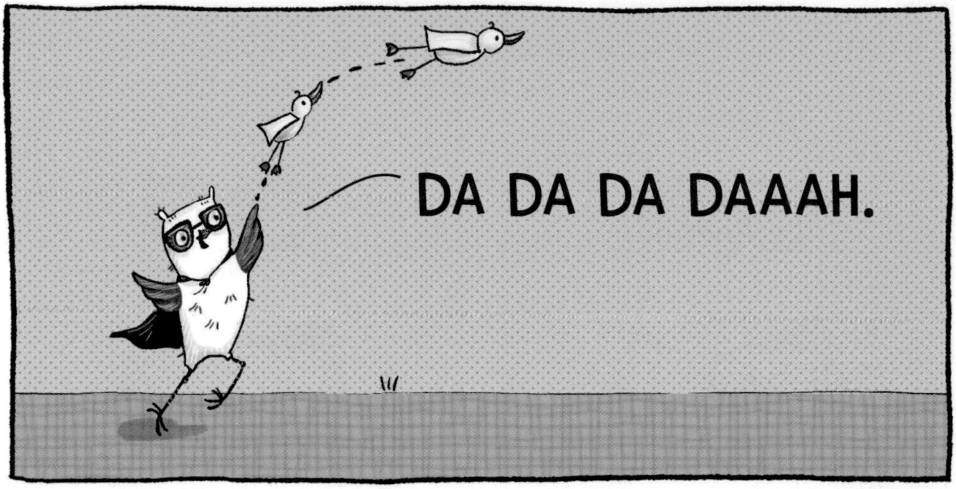
DA DA DA DAAAH.

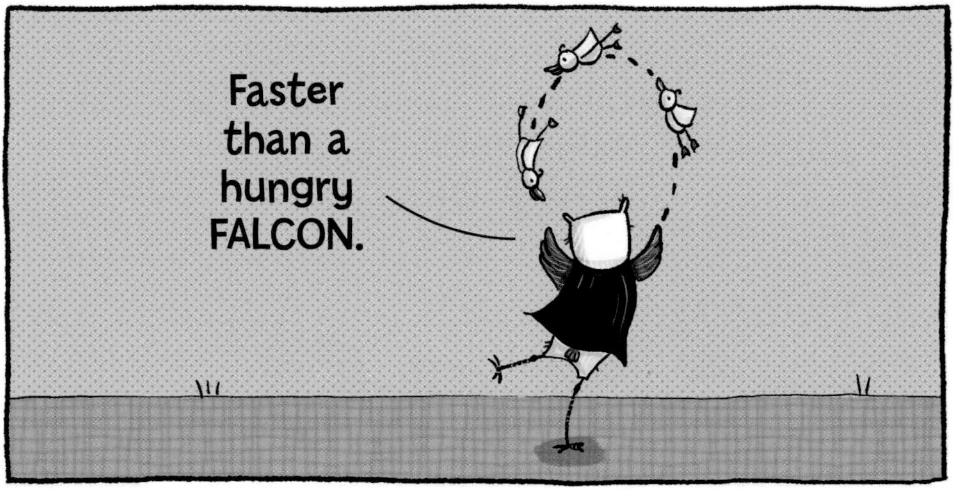
Faster than a hungry FALCON.

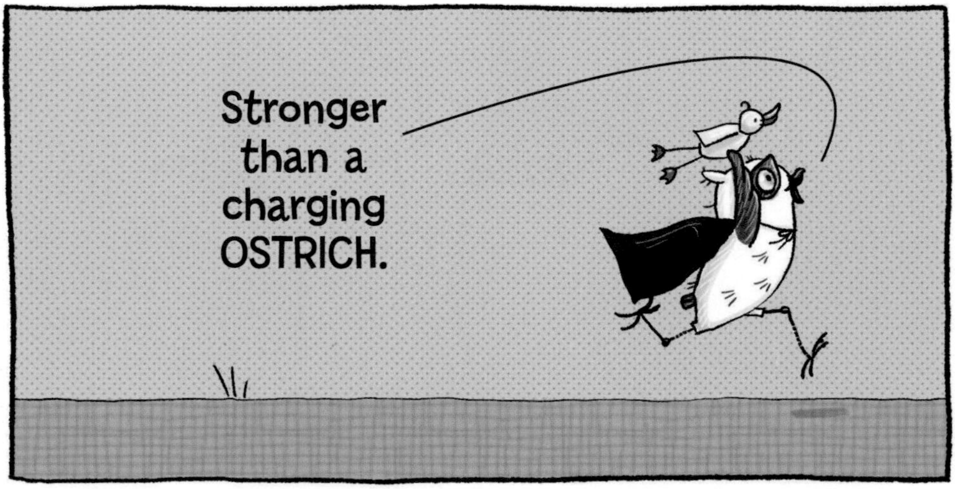
Stronger than a charging OSTRICH.

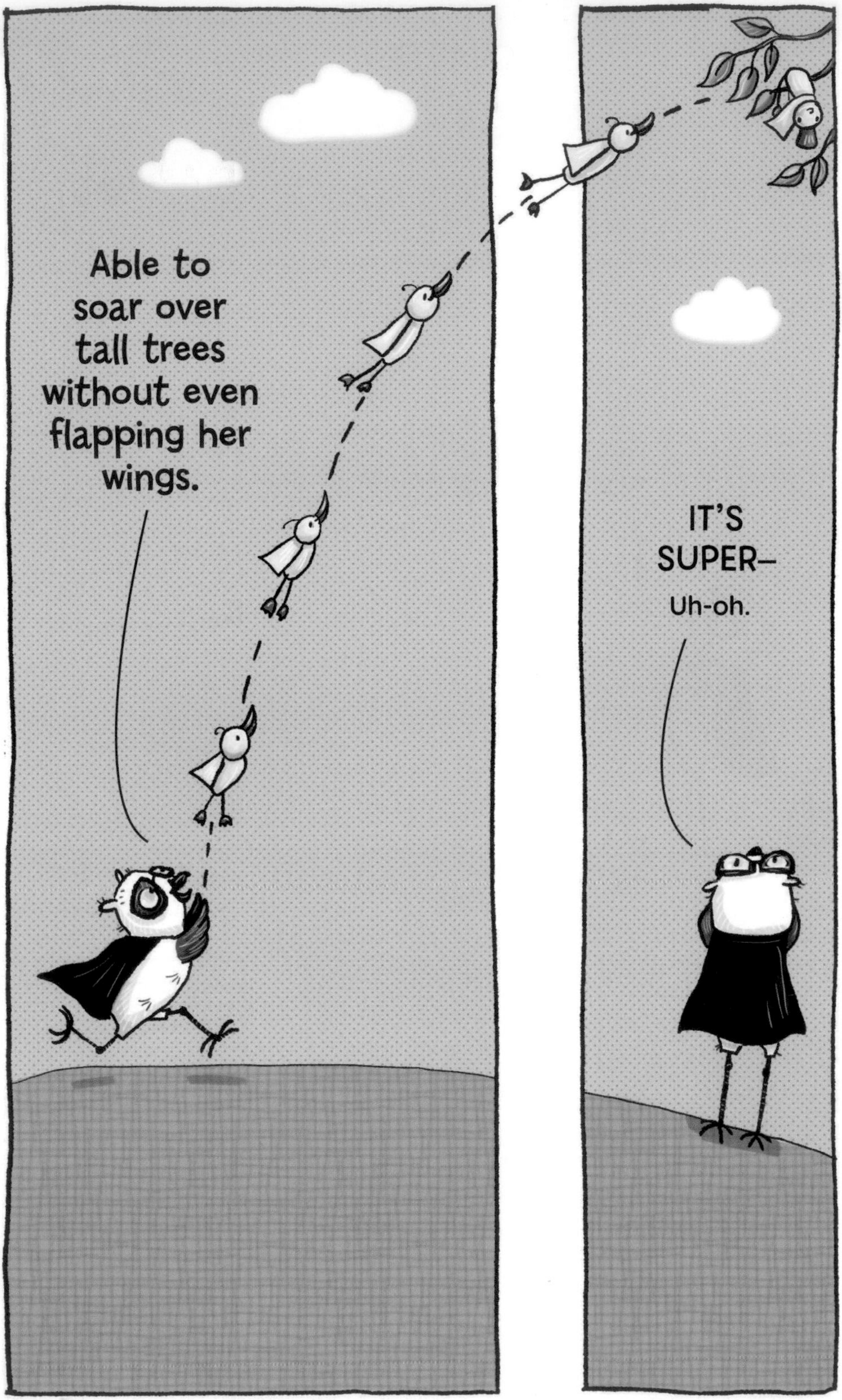
Able to soar over tall trees without even flapping her wings.
IT'S SUPER—
Uh-oh.

CHAPTER 2

CHUCK-A-DUCK

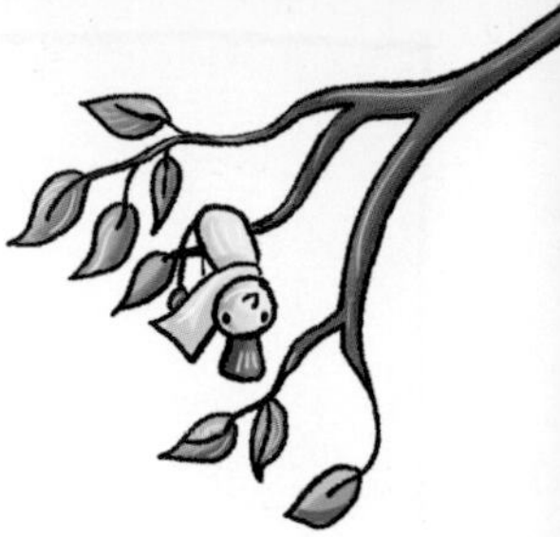

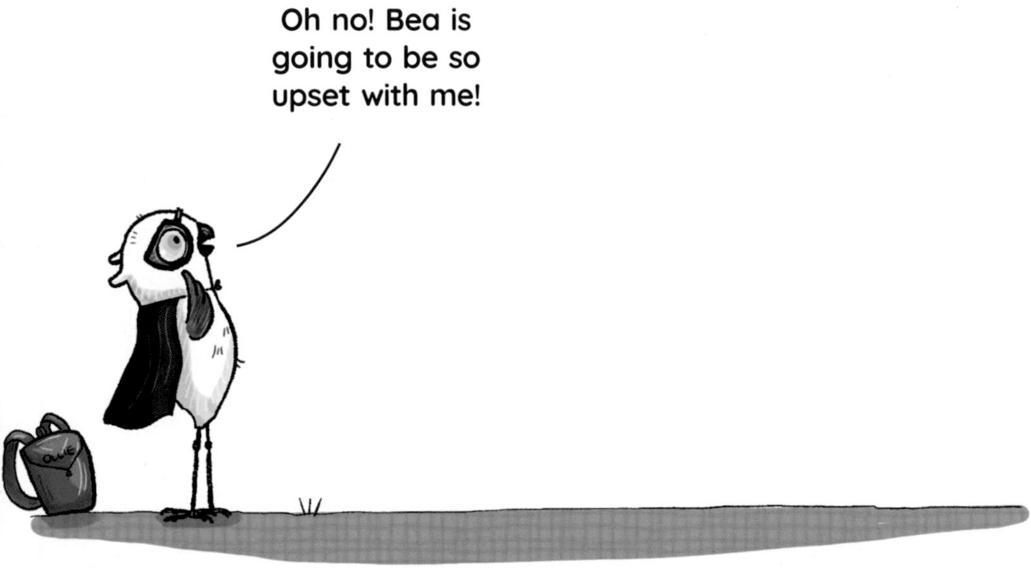
Oh no! Bea is going to be so upset with me!

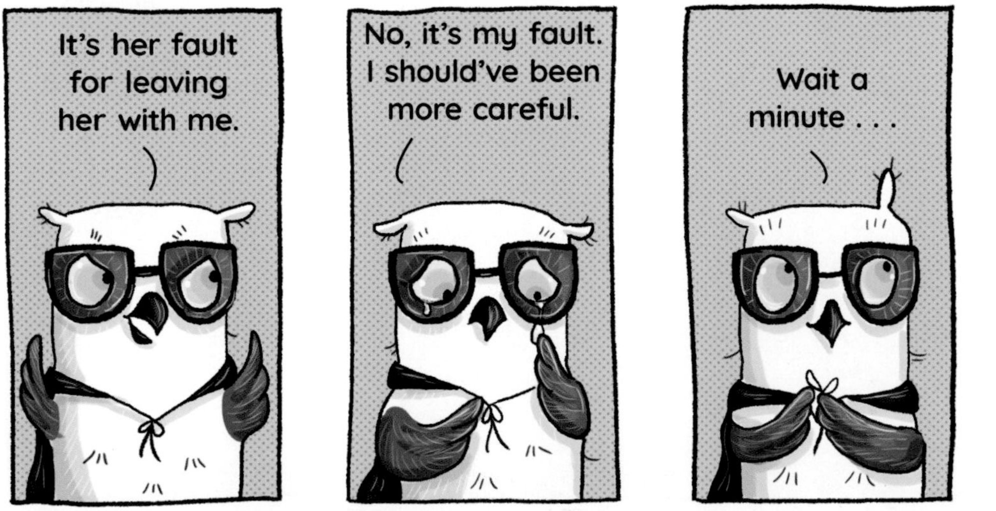
It's her fault for leaving her with me.
No, it's my fault. I should've been more careful.
Wait a minute . . .

Never fear, Super Duck . . .

Super Owl and his . . .

superlasso are here!

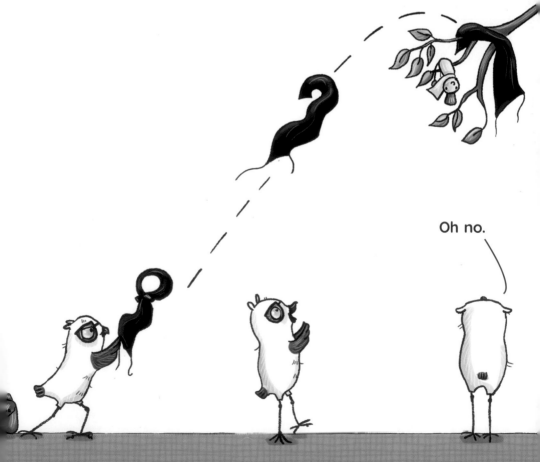

Oh no.

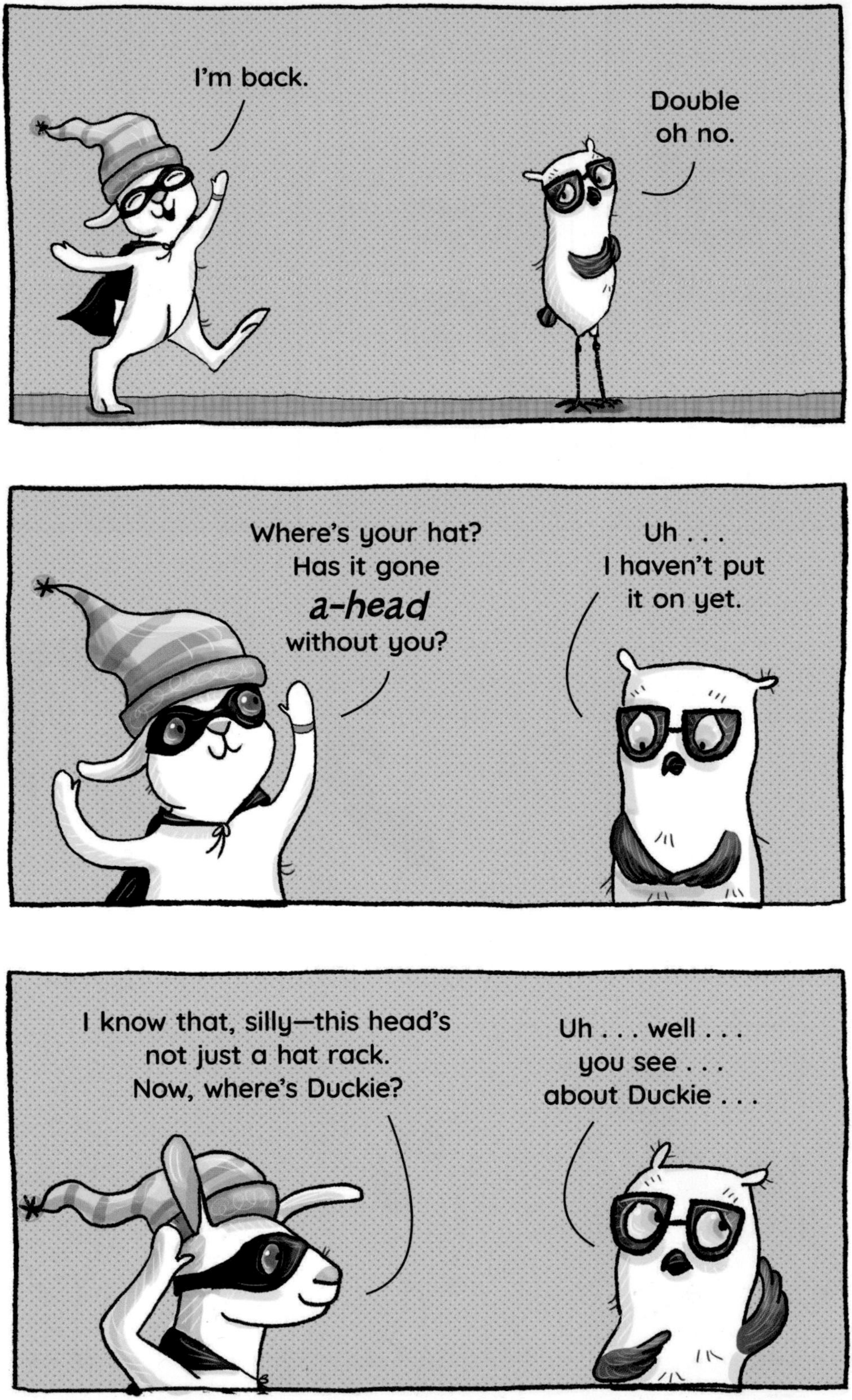
I'm back.
Double oh no.
Where's your hat? Has it gone *a-head* without you?
Uh . . . I haven't put it on yet.
I know that, silly—this head's not just a hat rack. Now, where's Duckie?
Uh . . . well . . . you see . . . about Duckie . . .

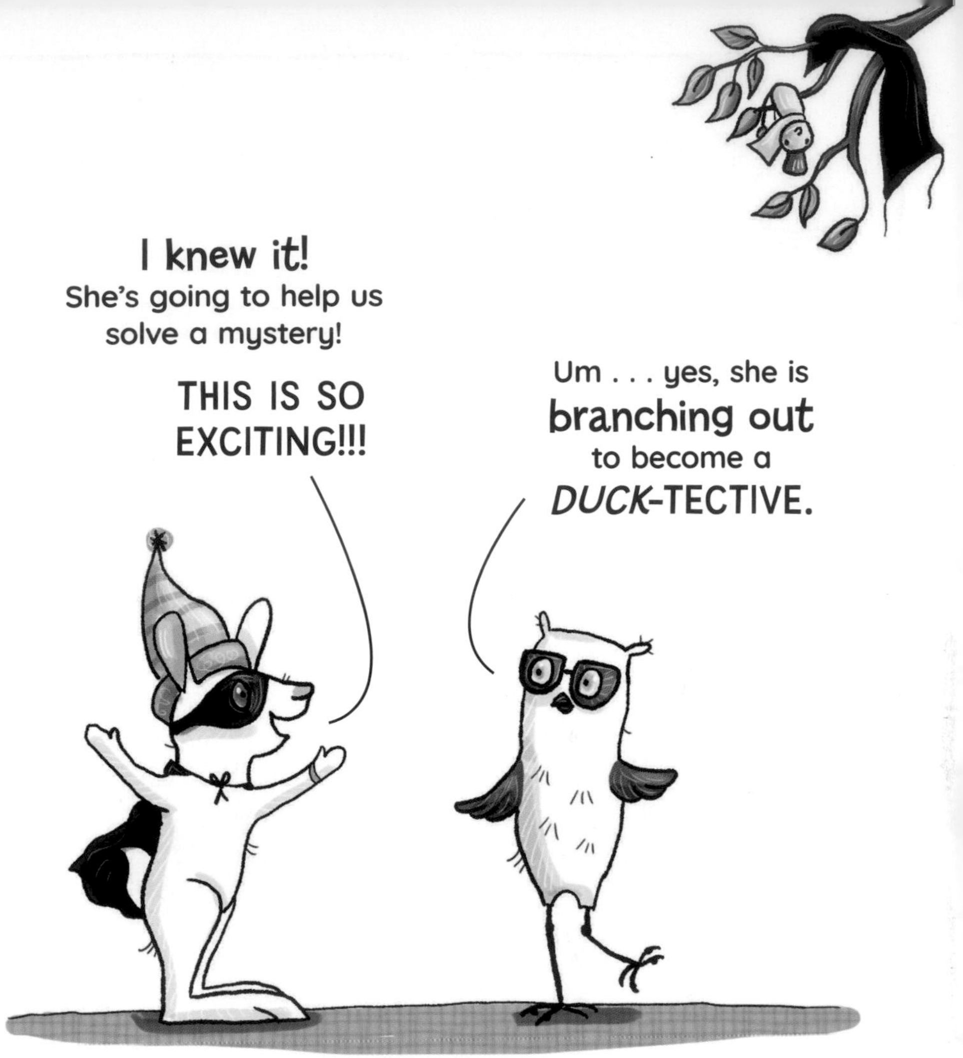
I knew it!
She's going to help us solve a mystery!
THIS IS SO EXCITING!!!
Um . . . yes, she is **branching out** to become a *DUCK*-TECTIVE.

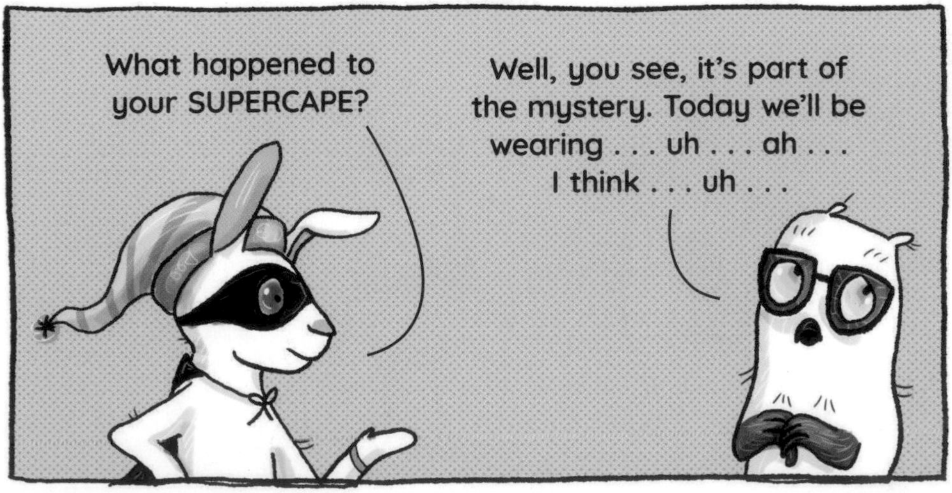
What happened to your SUPERCAPE?
Well, you see, it's part of the mystery. Today we'll be wearing . . . uh . . . ah . . . I think . . . uh . . .

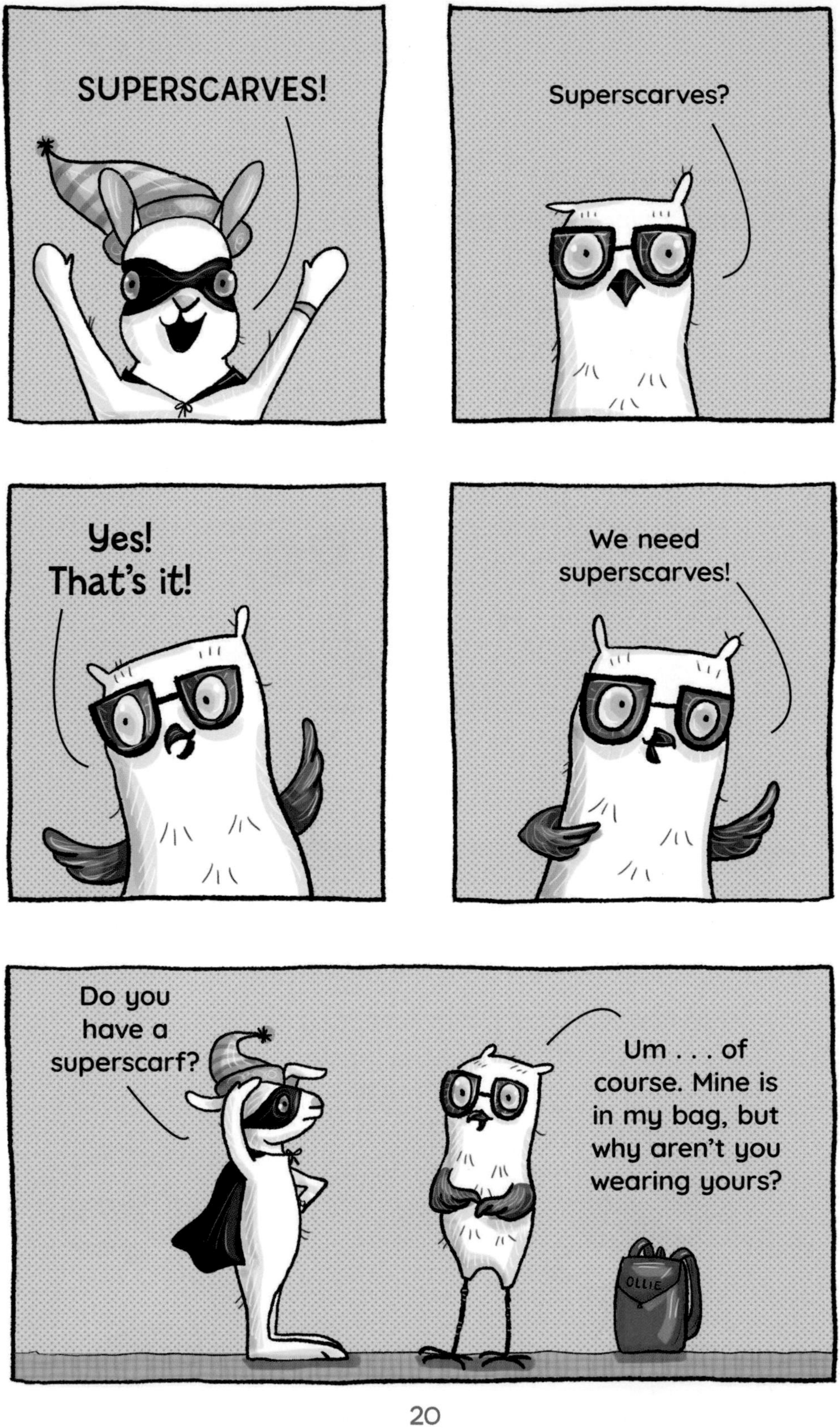
SUPERSCARVES!
Superscarves?
Yes! That's it!
We need superscarves!
Do you have a superscarf?
Um . . . of course. Mine is in my bag, but why aren't you wearing yours?
OLLIE

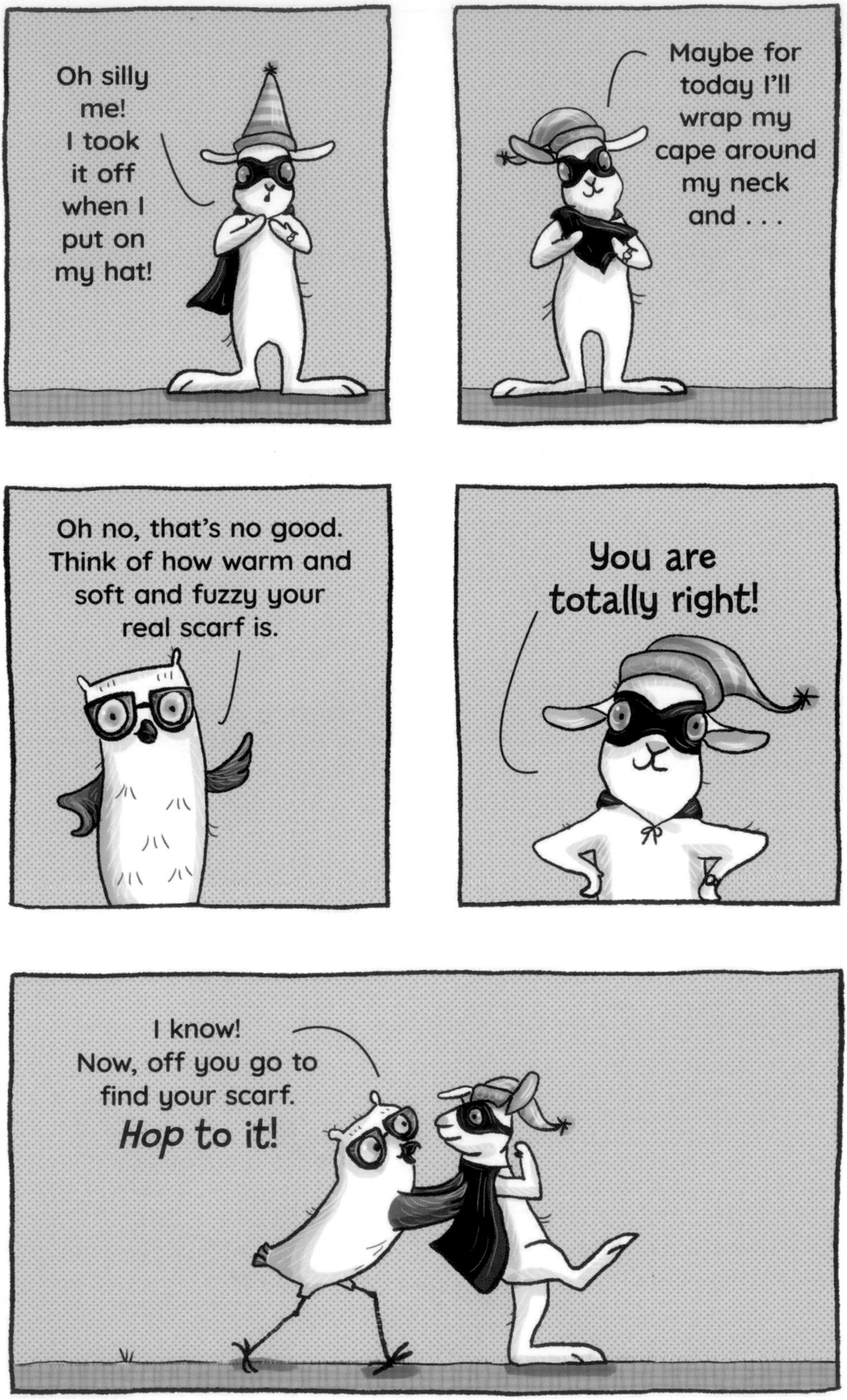
Oh silly me! I took it off when I put on my hat!
Maybe for today I'll wrap my cape around my neck and . . .
Oh no, that's no good. Think of how warm and soft and fuzzy your real scarf is.
You are totally right!
I know! Now, off you go to find your scarf. *Hop* to it!

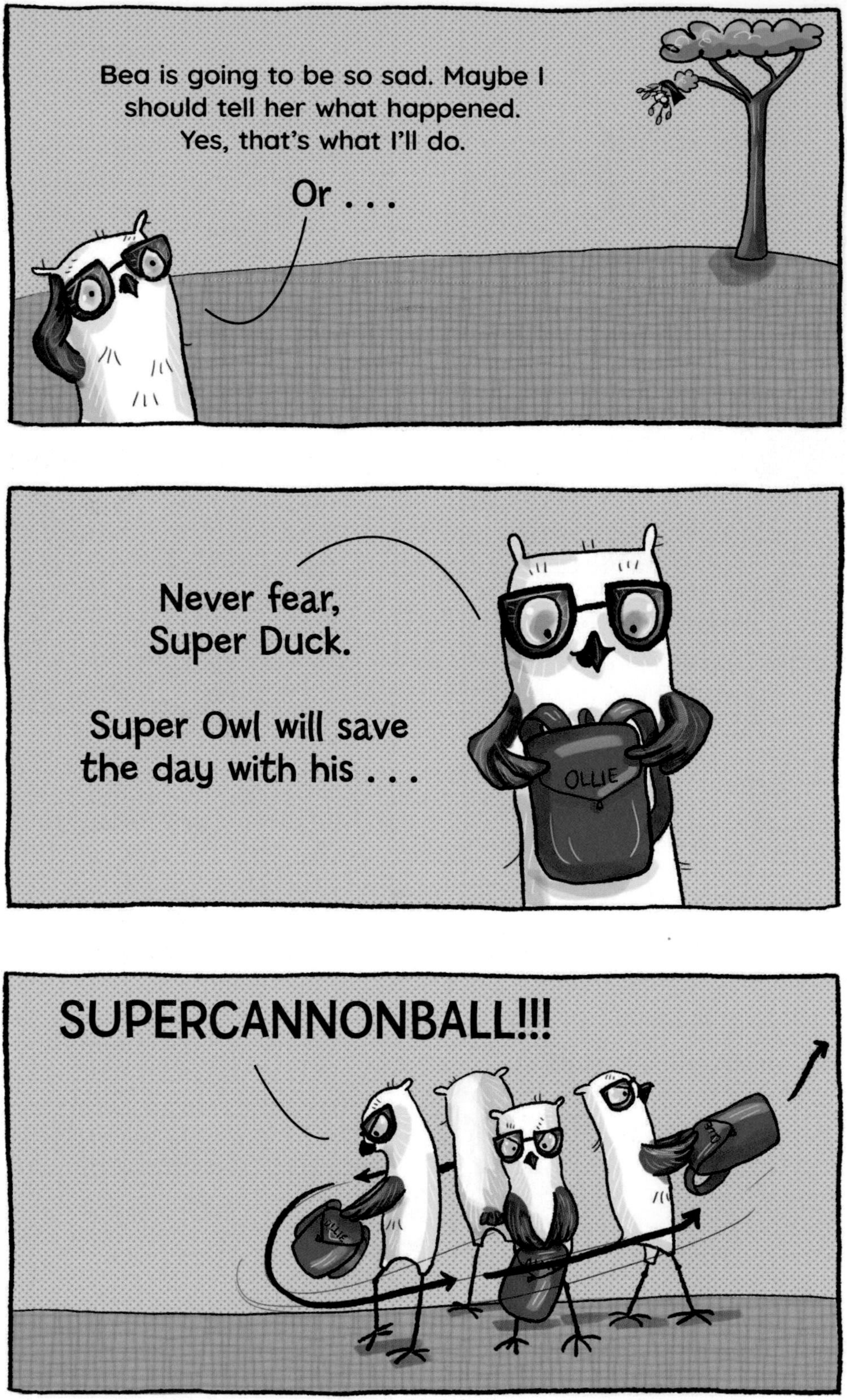
Bea is going to be so sad. Maybe I should tell her what happened. Yes, that's what I'll do.
Or . . .
Never fear, Super Duck.
Super Owl will save the day with his . . .
OLLIE
SUPERCANNONBALL!!!

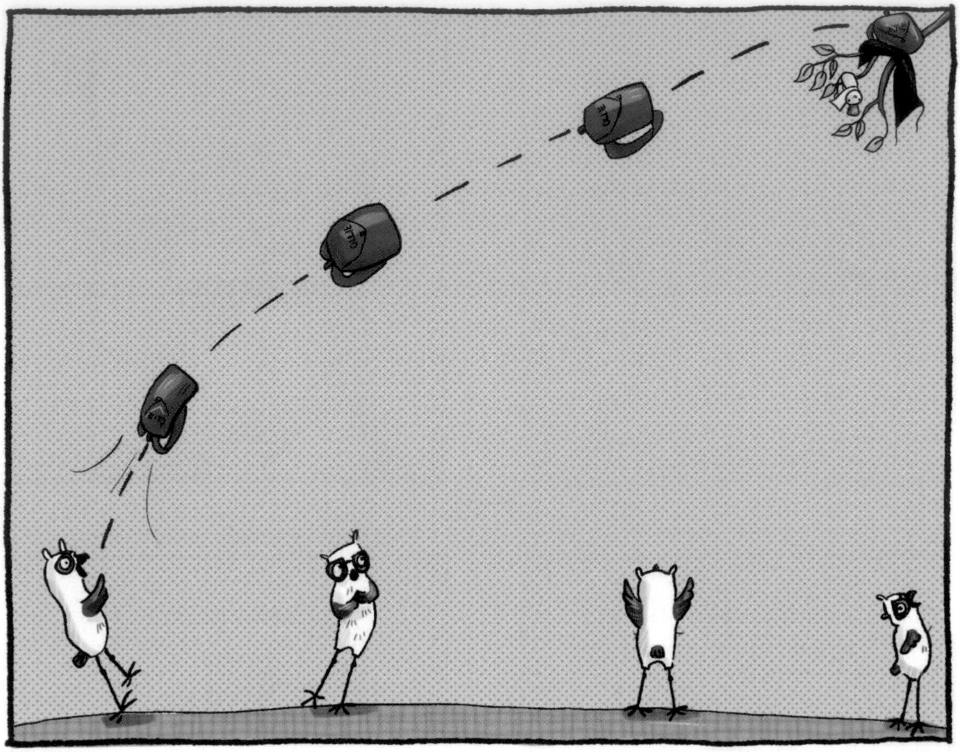

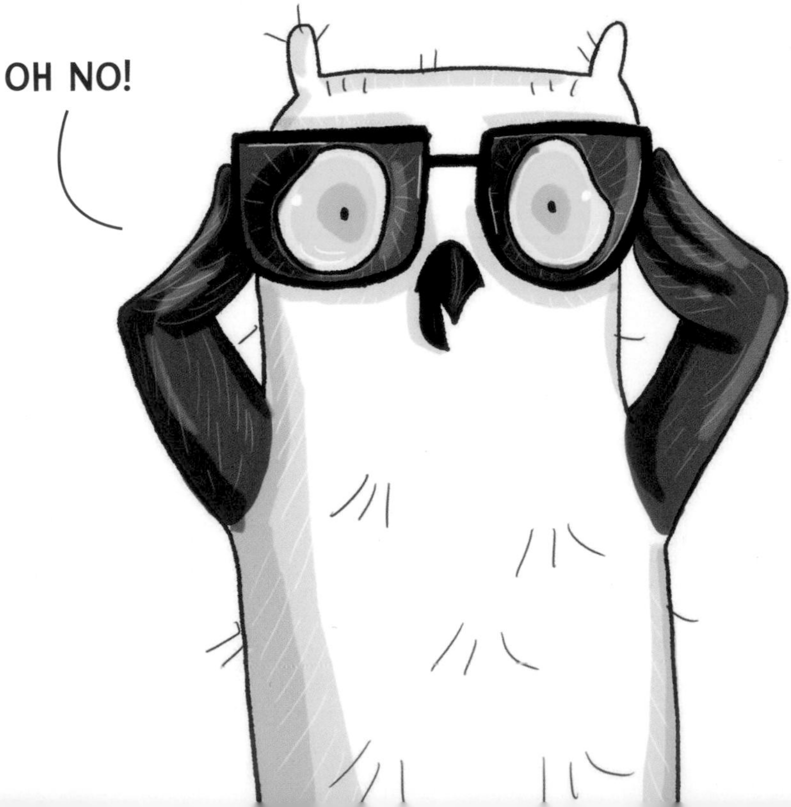
OH NO!

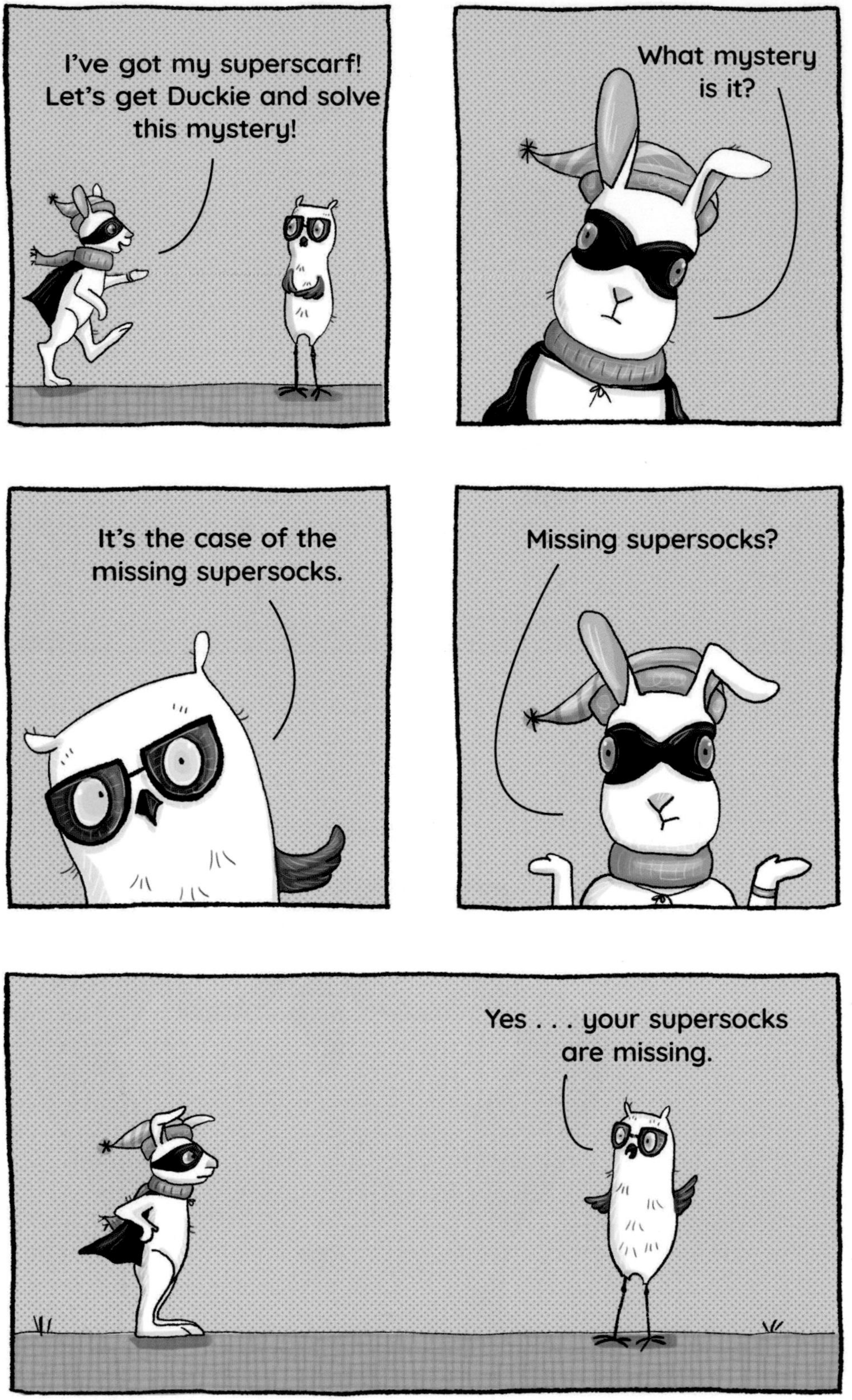
I've got my superscarf! Let's get Duckie and solve this mystery!
What mystery is it?
It's the case of the missing supersocks.
Missing supersocks?
Yes . . . your supersocks are missing.

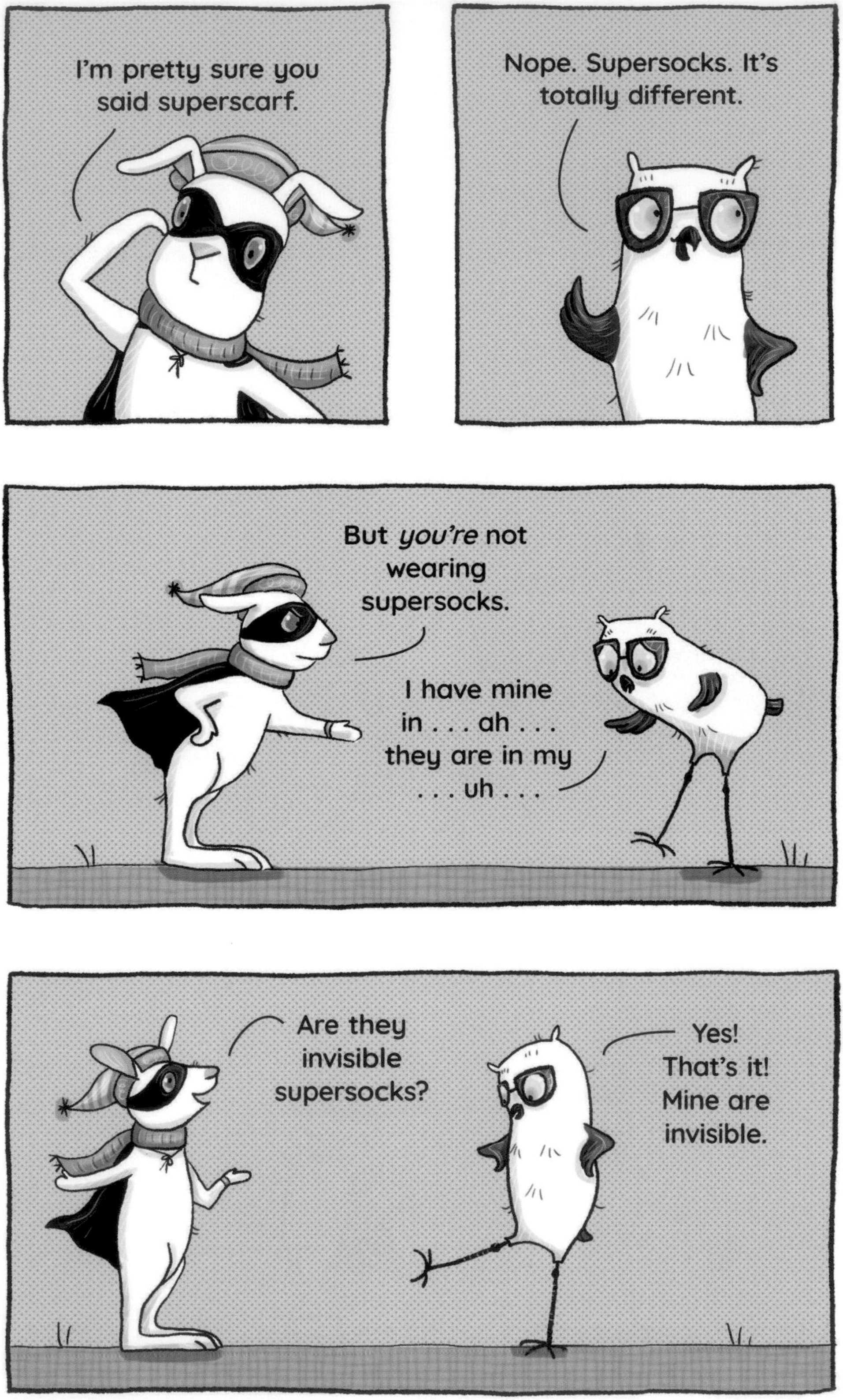
I'm pretty sure you said superscarf.
Nope. Supersocks. It's totally different.
But *you're* not wearing supersocks.
I have mine in . . . ah . . . they are in my . . . uh . . .
Are they invisible supersocks?
Yes! That's it! Mine are invisible.

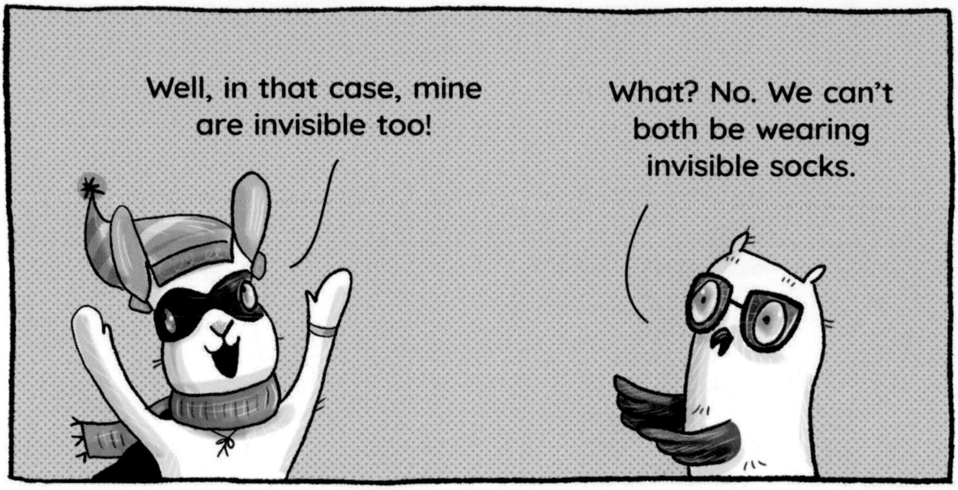
Well, in that case, mine are invisible too!
What? No. We can't both be wearing invisible socks.

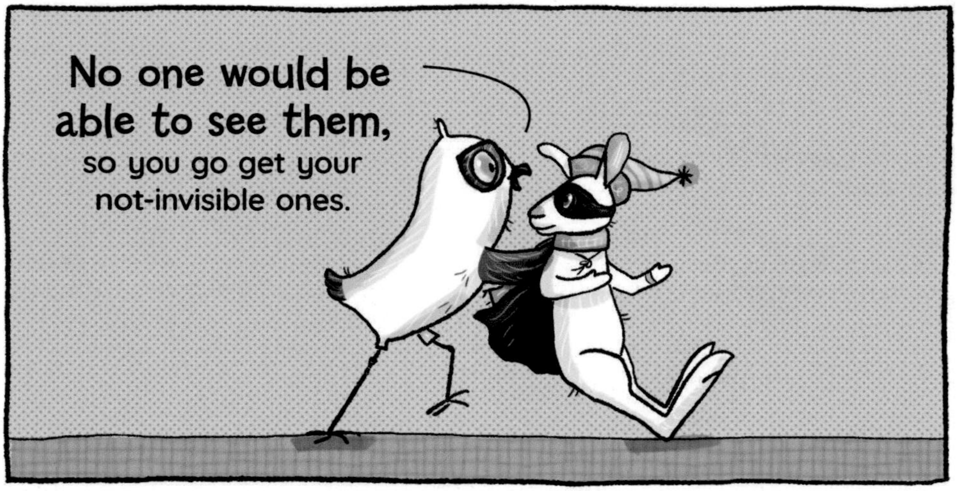
No one would be able to see them, so you go get your not-invisible ones.

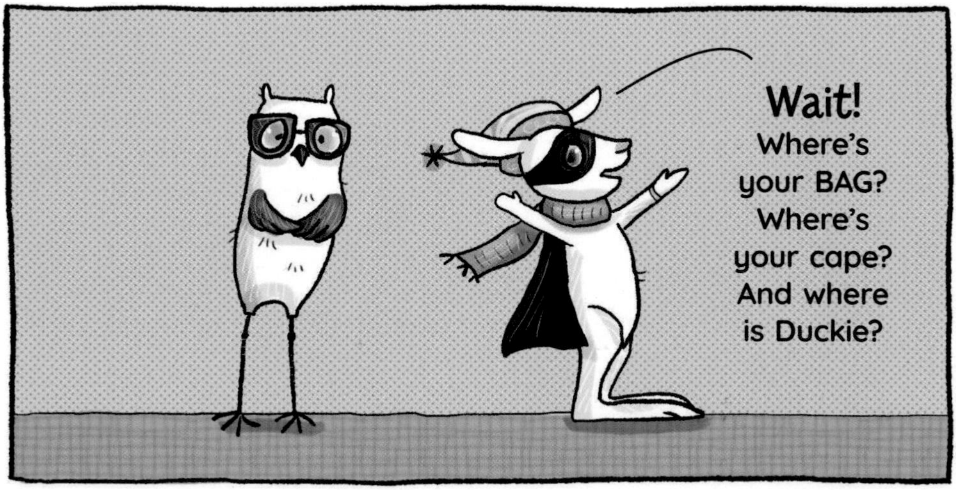
Wait! Where's your BAG? Where's your cape? And where is Duckie?

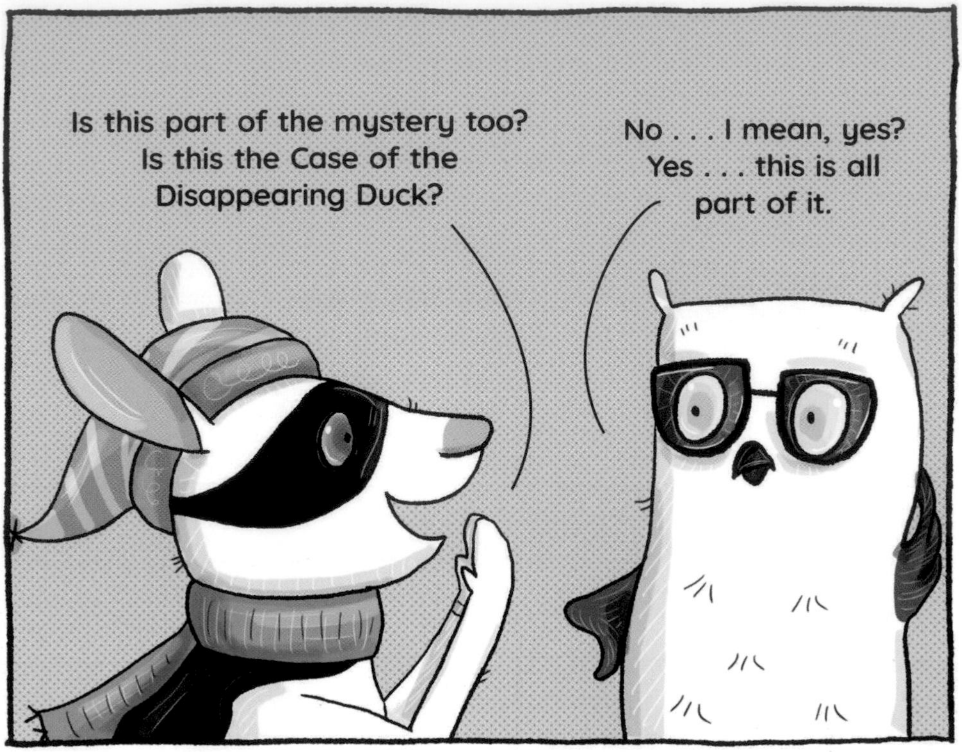
Is this part of the mystery too? Is this the Case of the Disappearing Duck?
No . . . I mean, yes? Yes . . . this is all part of it.

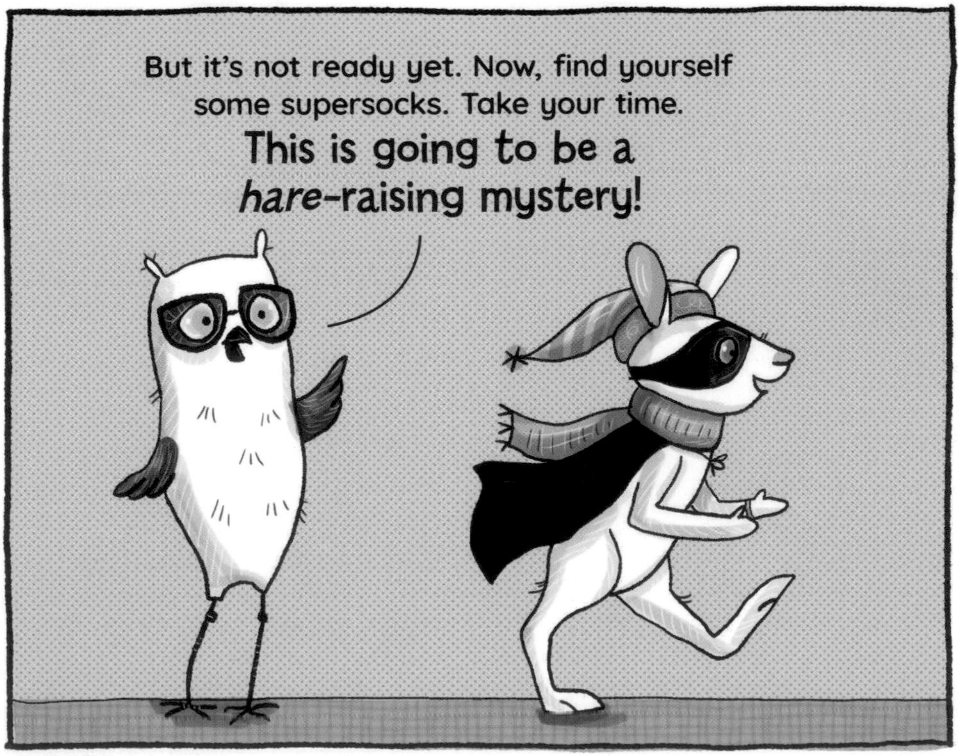
But it's not ready yet. Now, find yourself some supersocks. Take your time.
This is going to be a *hare*-raising mystery!

CHAPTER 3

SOCK HOP

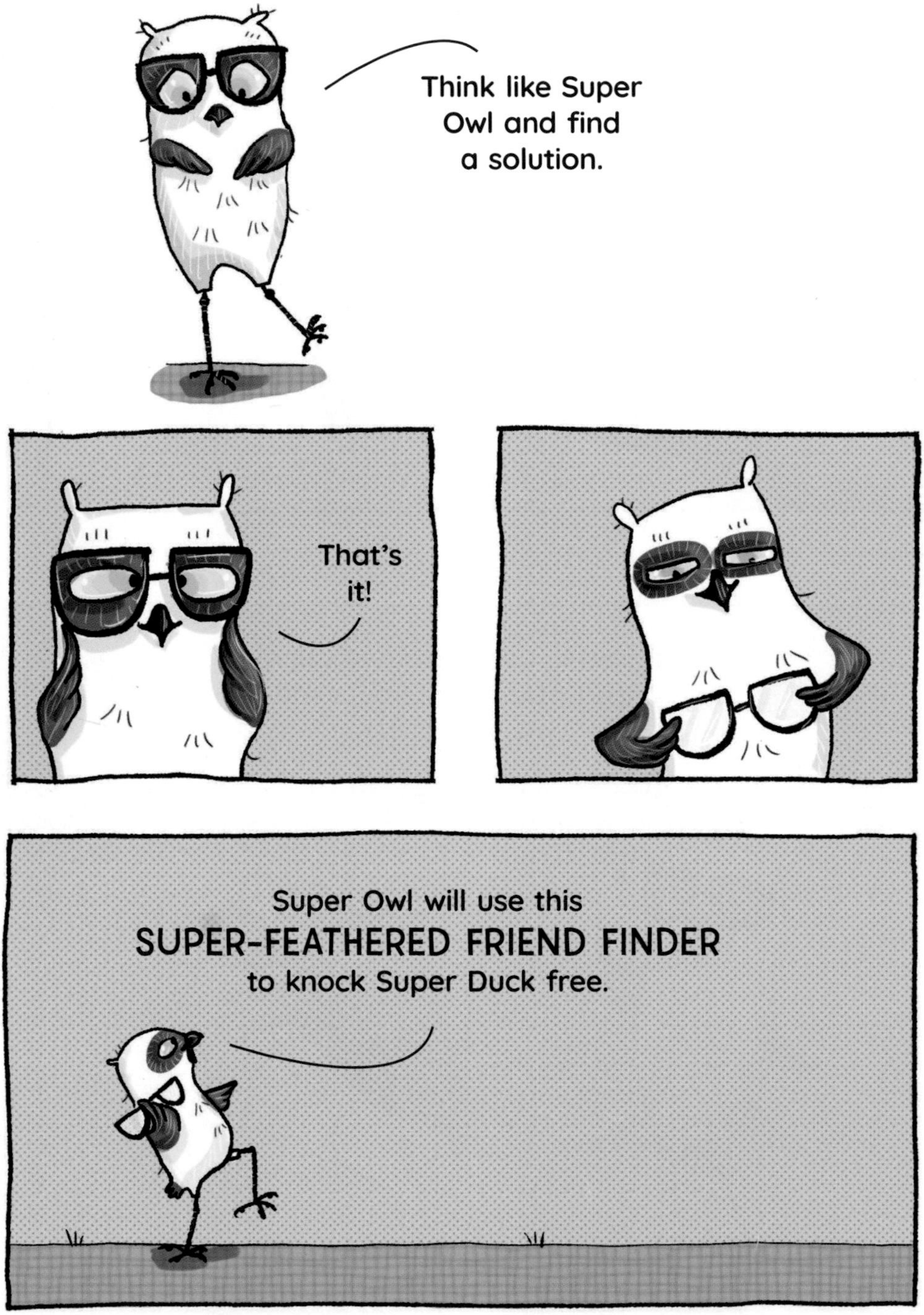
Think like Super Owl and find a solution.
That's it!
Super Owl will use this
SUPER-FEATHERED FRIEND FINDER
to knock Super Duck free.

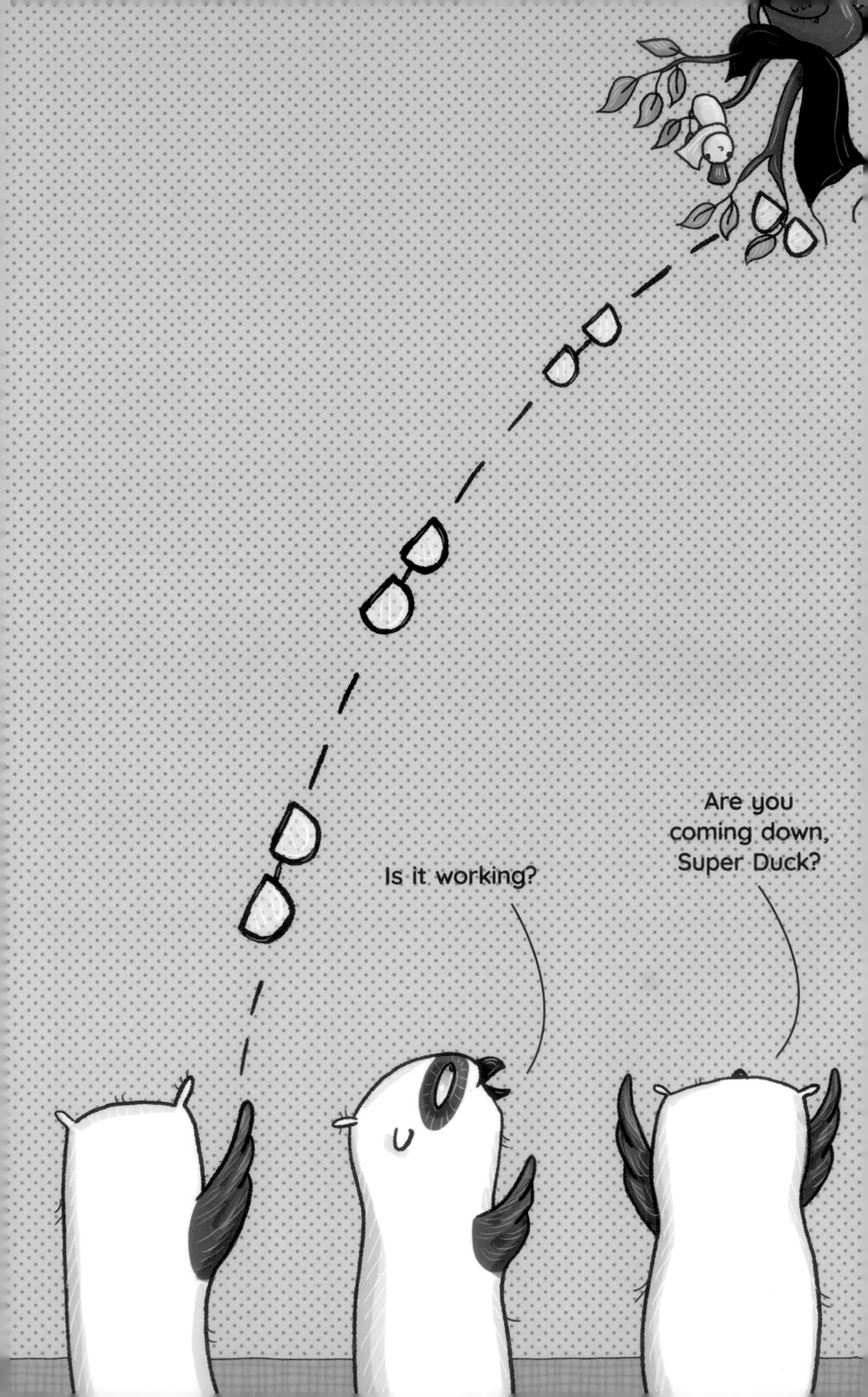
Is it working?
Are you coming down, Super Duck?

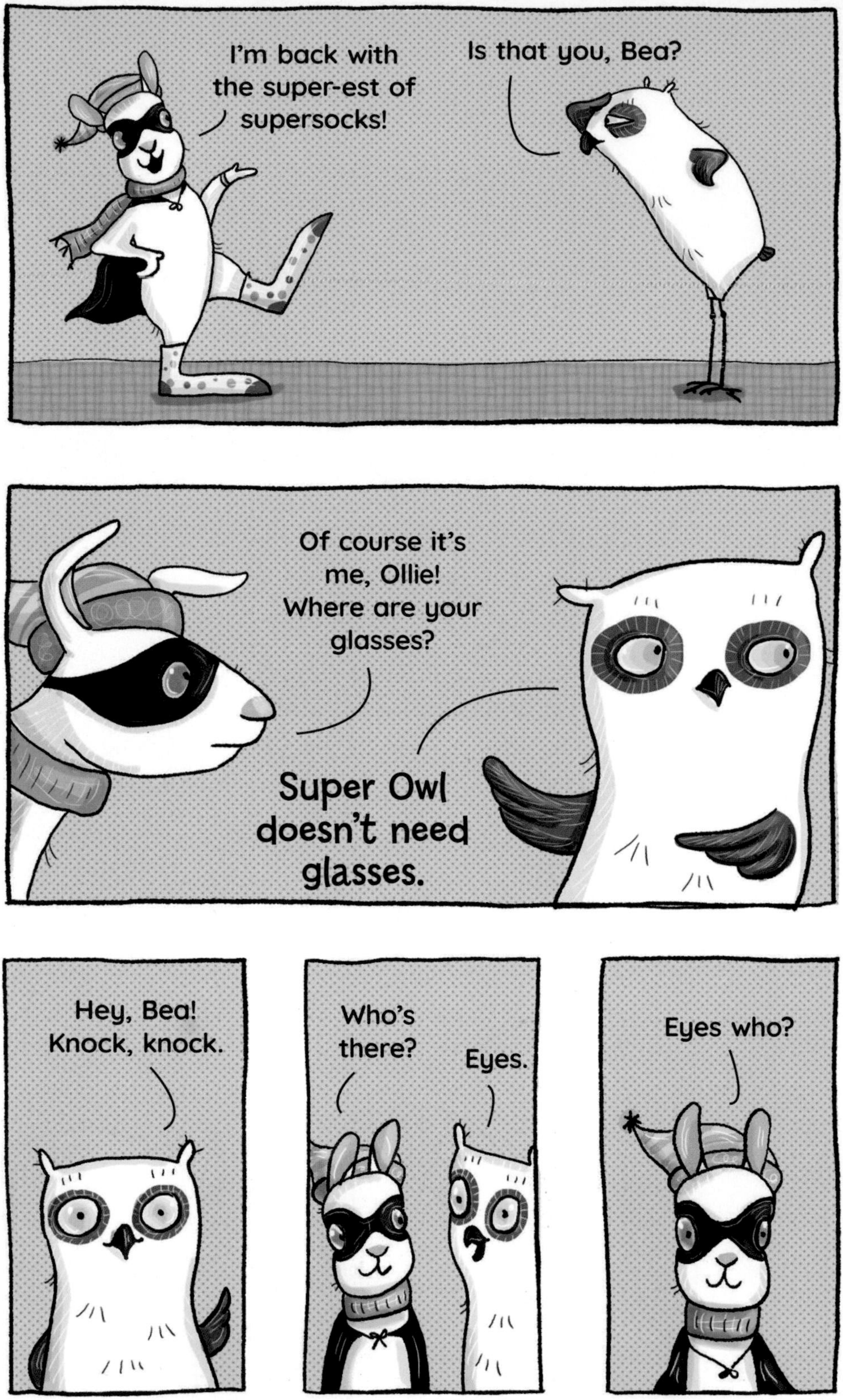
I'm back with the super-est of supersocks!
Is that you, Bea?
Of course it's me, Ollie! Where are your glasses?
Super Owl doesn't need glasses.
Hey, Bea! Knock, knock.
Who's there?
Eyes.
Eyes who?

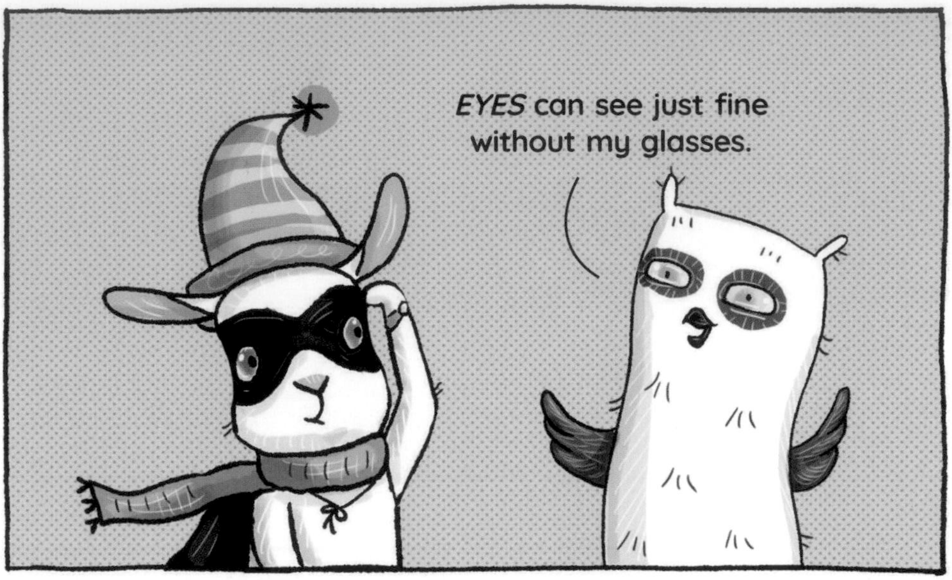
EYES can see just fine without my glasses.

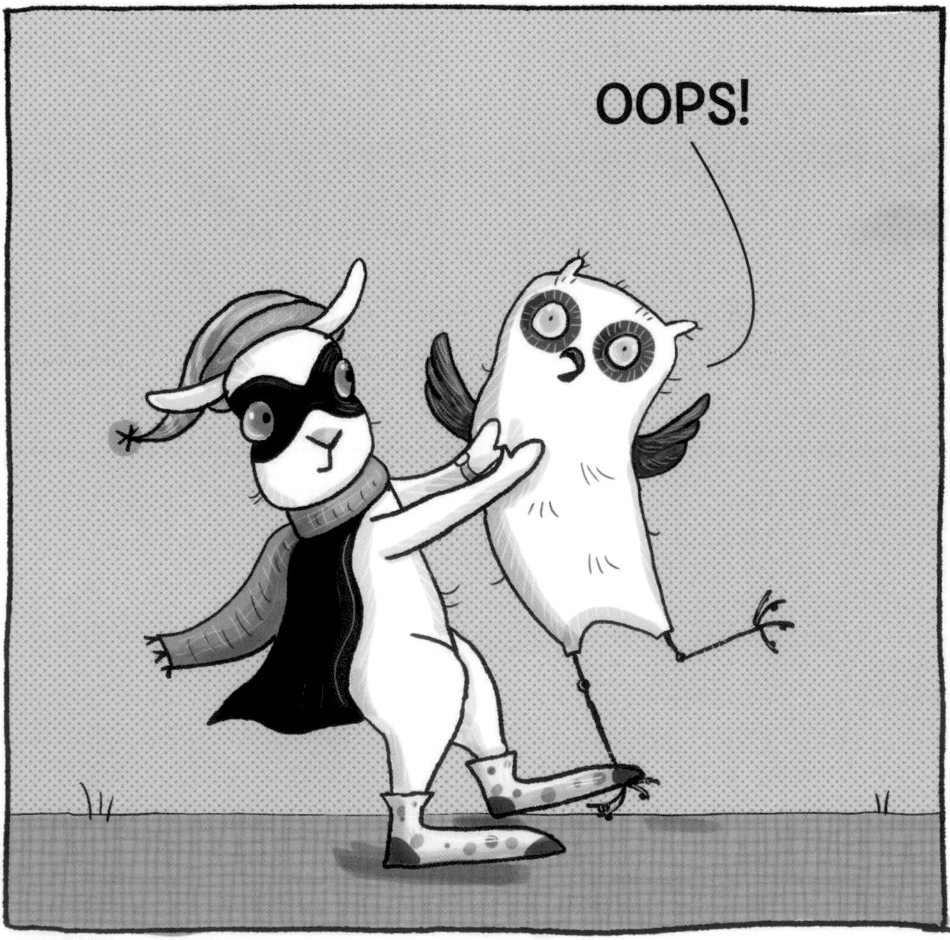
OOPS!

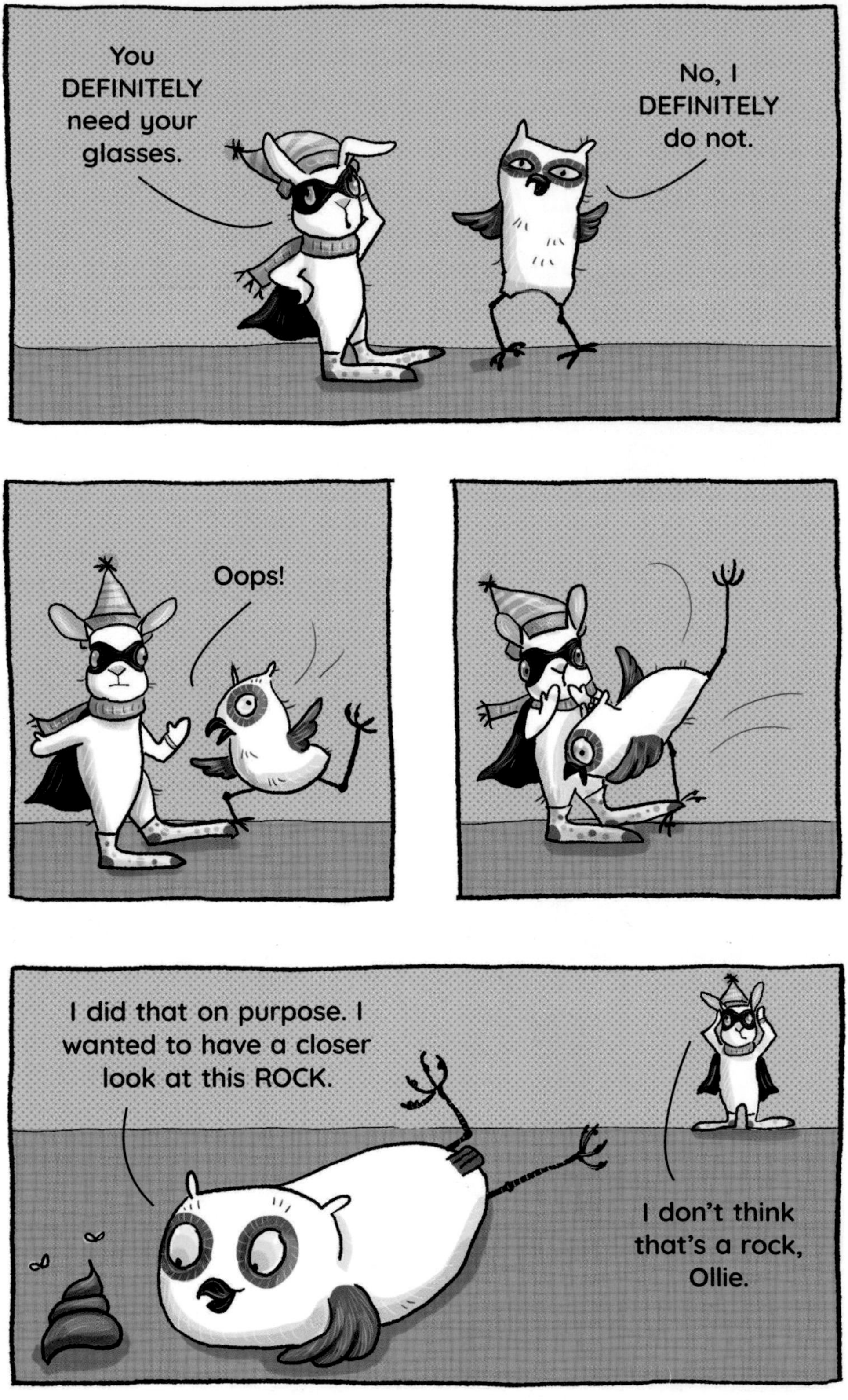
You DEFINITELY need your glasses.
No, I DEFINITELY do not.
Oops!
I did that on purpose. I wanted to have a closer look at this ROCK.
I don't think that's a rock, Ollie.

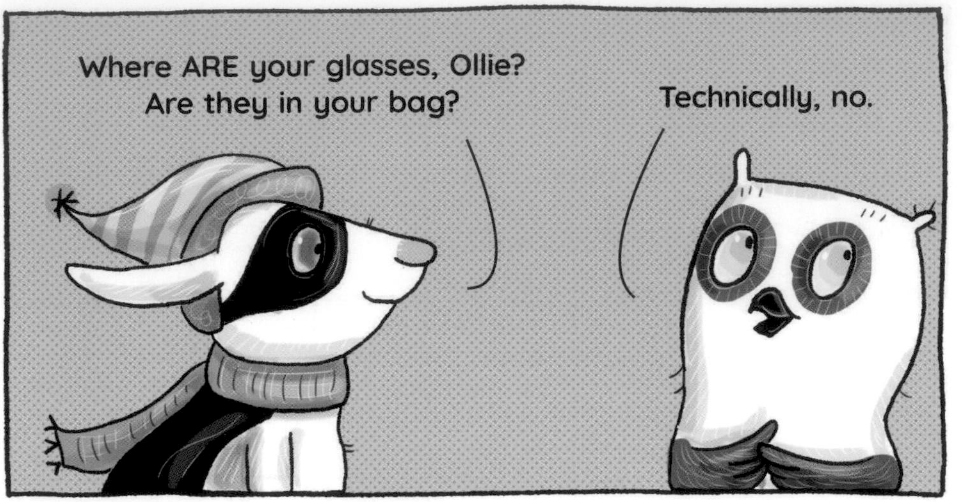
Where ARE your glasses, Ollie?
Are they in your bag?
Technically, no.

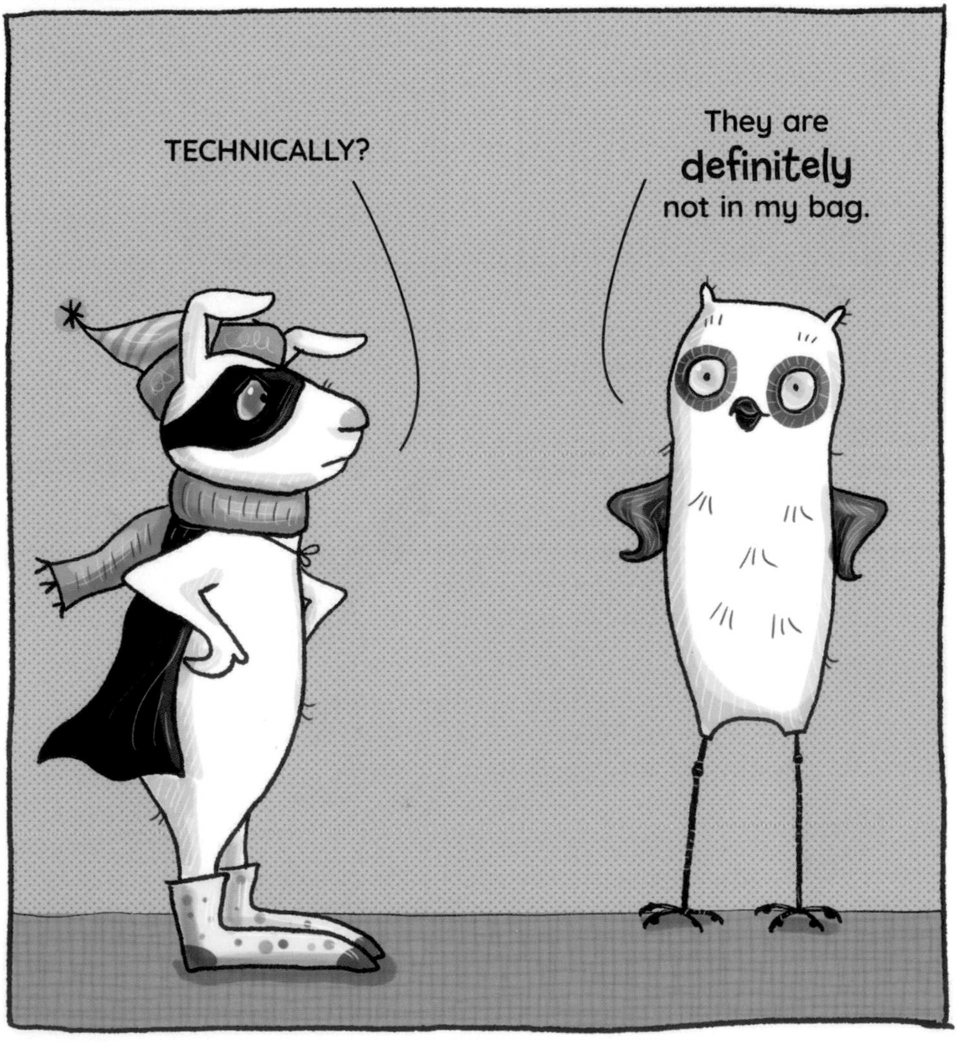
TECHNICALLY?
They are **definitely** not in my bag.

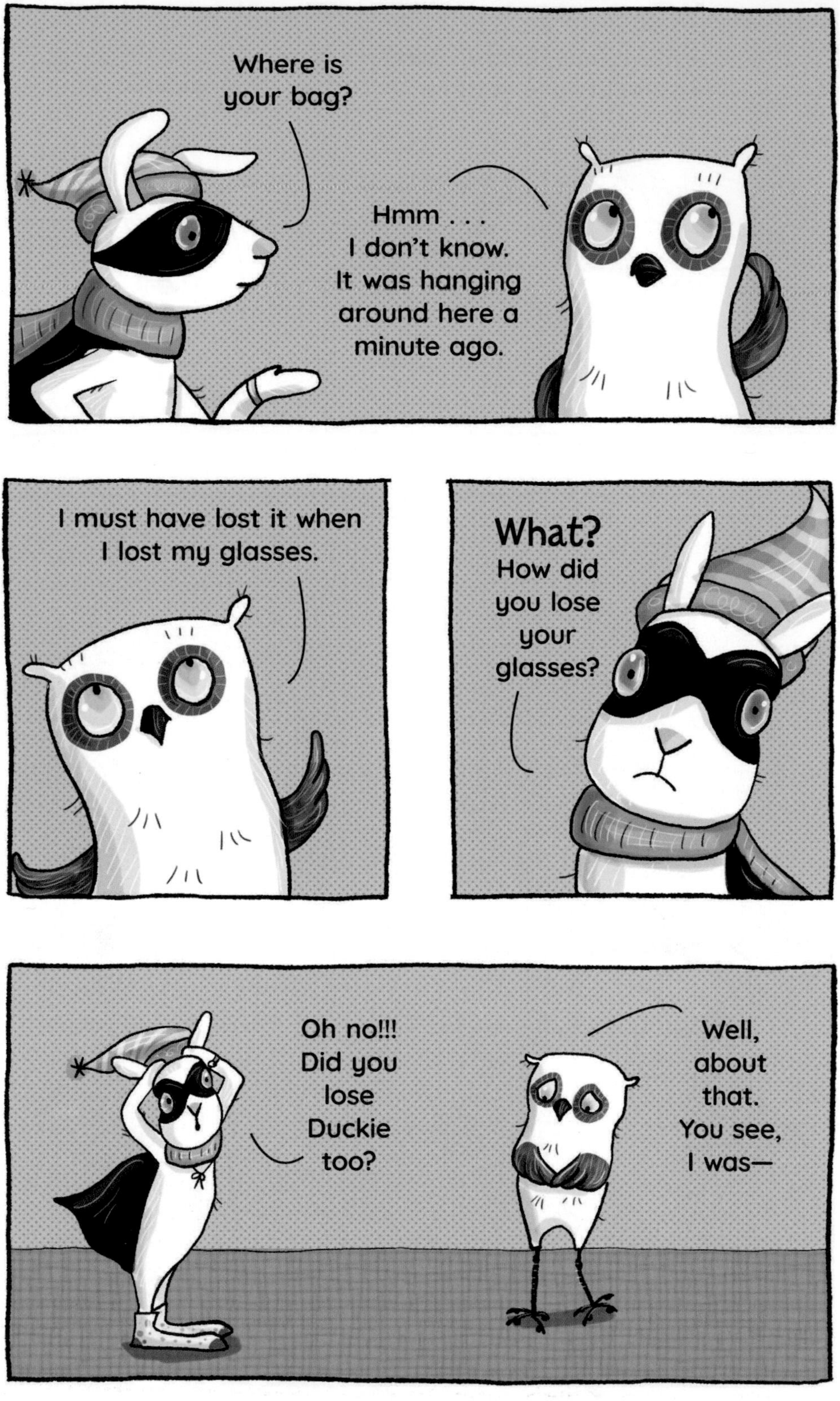
Where is your bag?
Hmm . . . I don't know. It was hanging around here a minute ago.
I must have lost it when I lost my glasses.
What? How did you lose your glasses?
Oh no!!! Did you lose Duckie too?
Well, about that. You see, I was—

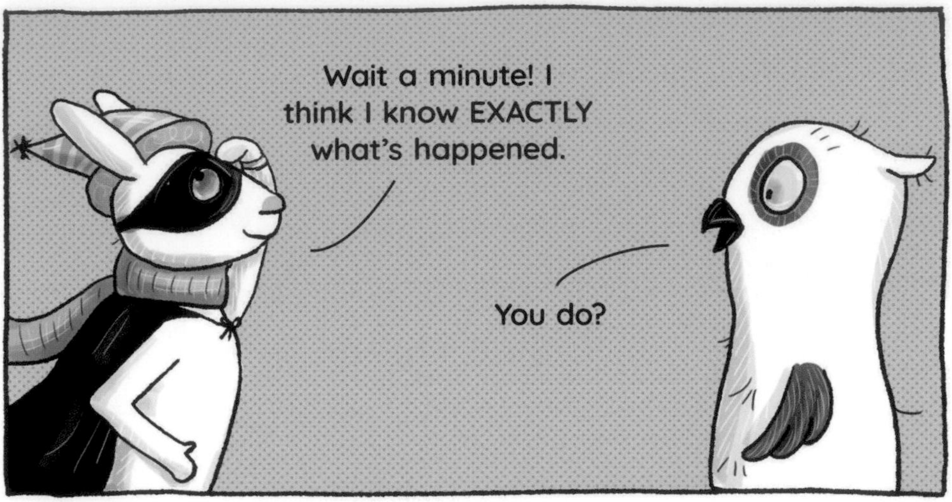
Wait a minute! I think I know EXACTLY what's happened.
You do?

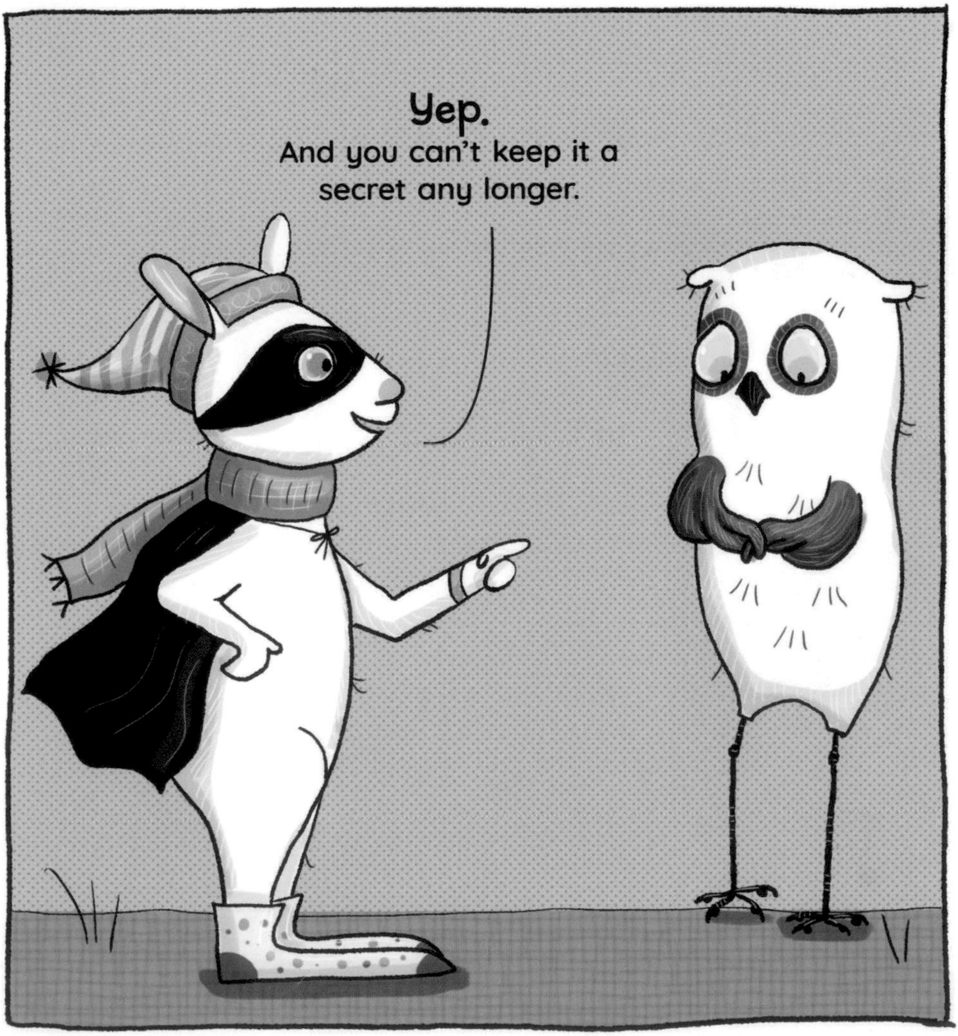
Yep.
And you can't keep it a secret any longer.

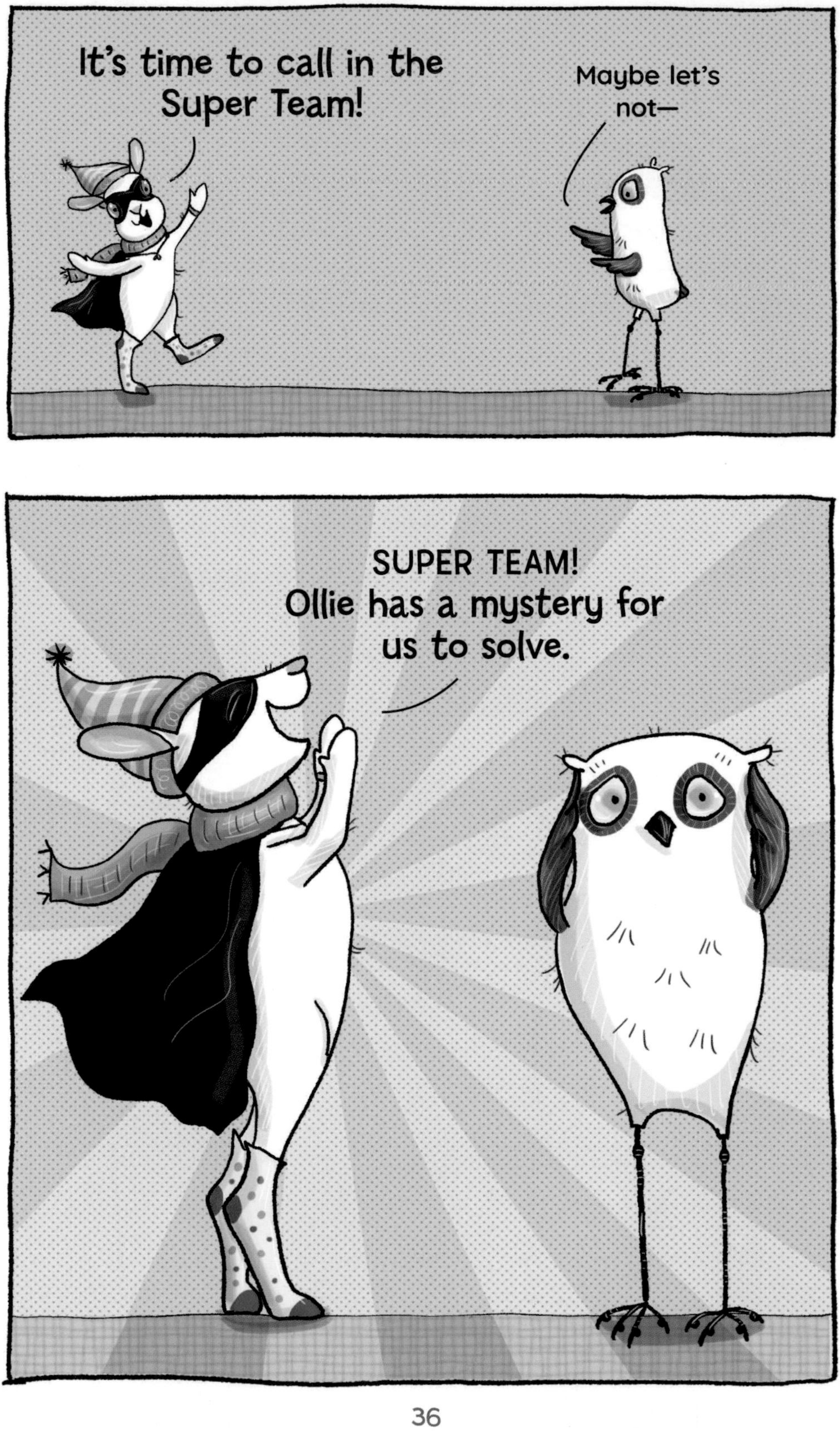
It's time to call in the Super Team!
Maybe let's not—
SUPER TEAM! Ollie has a mystery for us to solve.

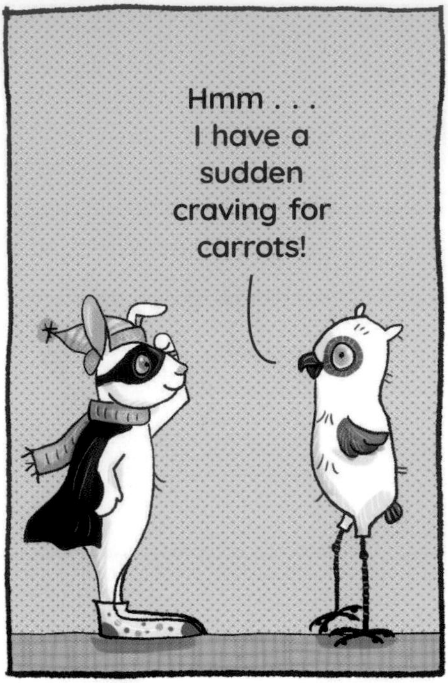
Hmm . . . I have a sudden craving for carrots!

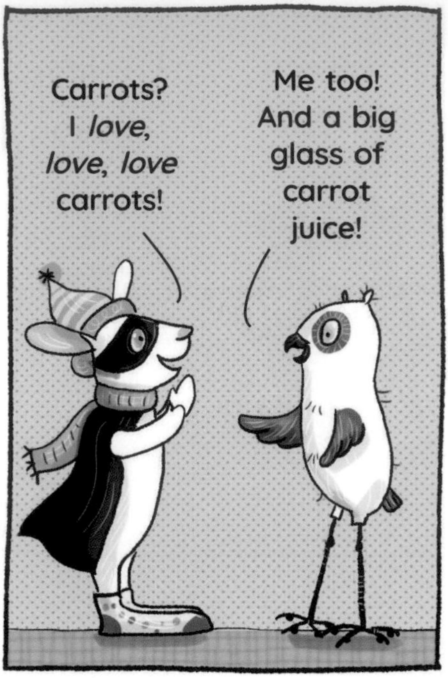
Carrots? I *love*, *love*, *love* carrots!
Me too! And a big glass of carrot juice!

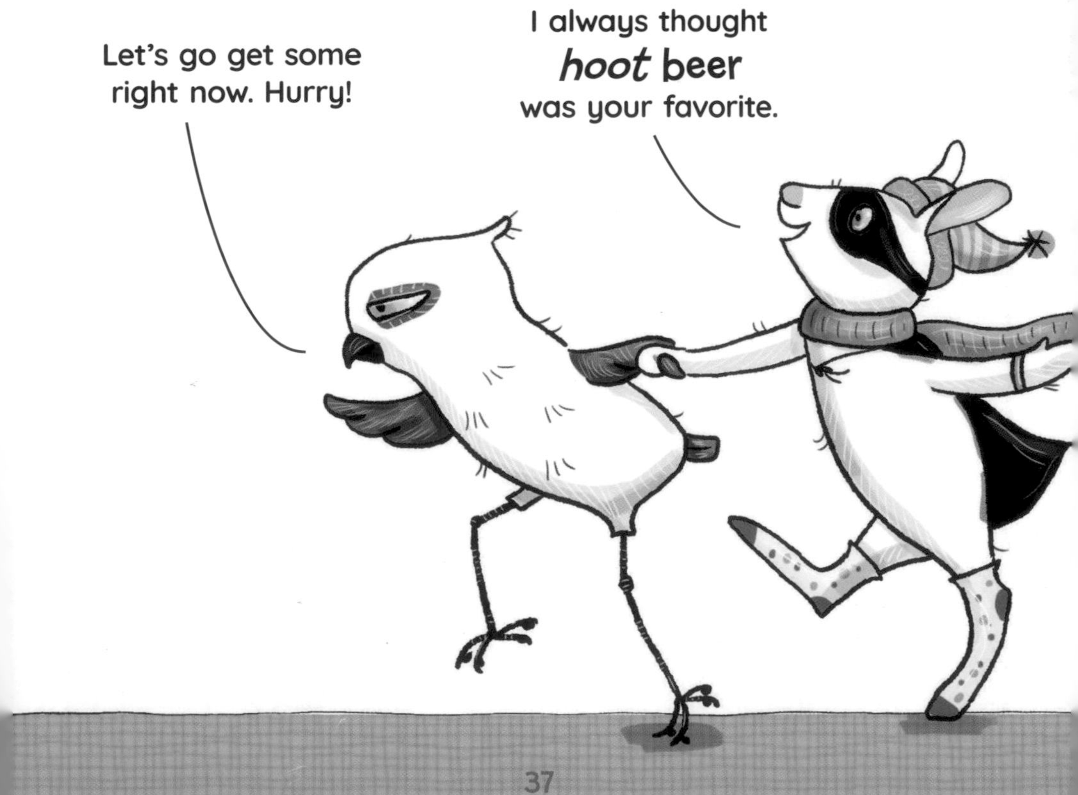
Let's go get some right now. Hurry!
I always thought ***hoot*** **beer** was your favorite.

CHAPTER 4
HOO-DUNNIT

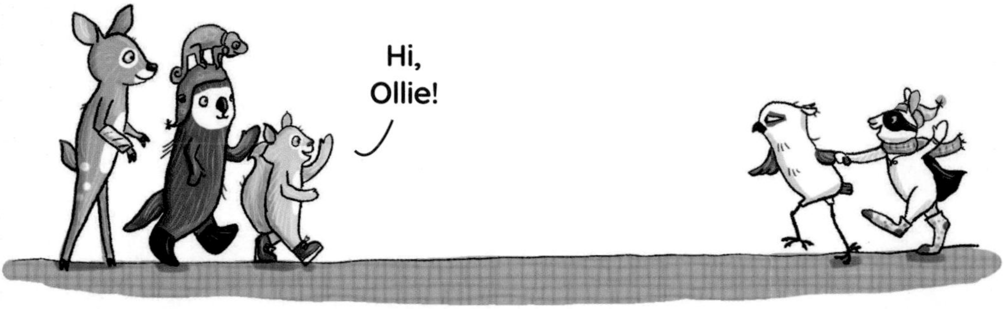
Hi,
Ollie!

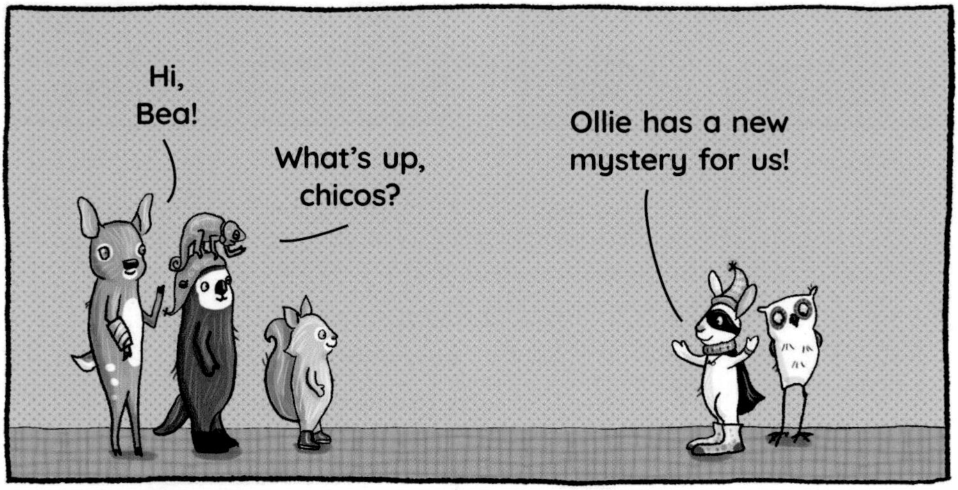
Hi,
Bea!
What's up,
chicos?
Ollie has a new
mystery for us!

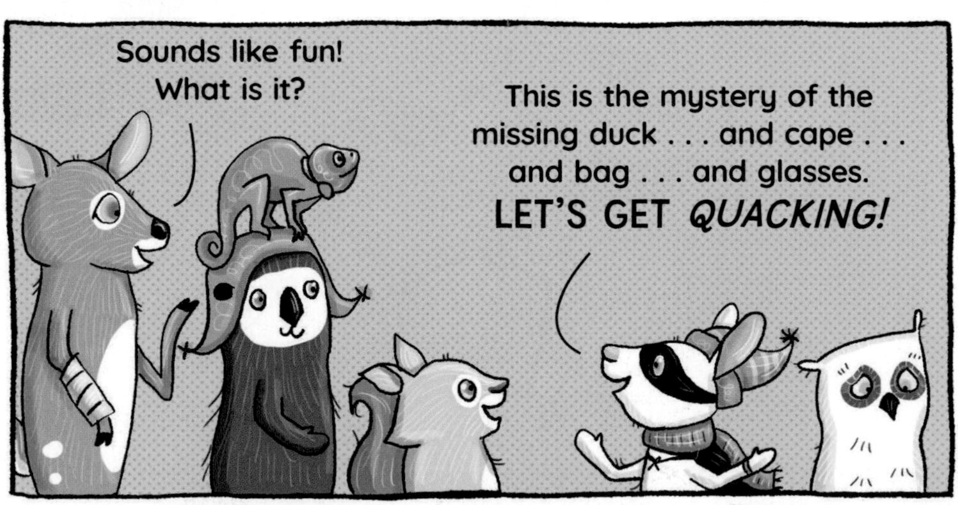
Sounds like fun!
What is it?
This is the mystery of the
missing duck . . . and cape . . .
and bag . . . and glasses.
LET'S GET *QUACKING!*

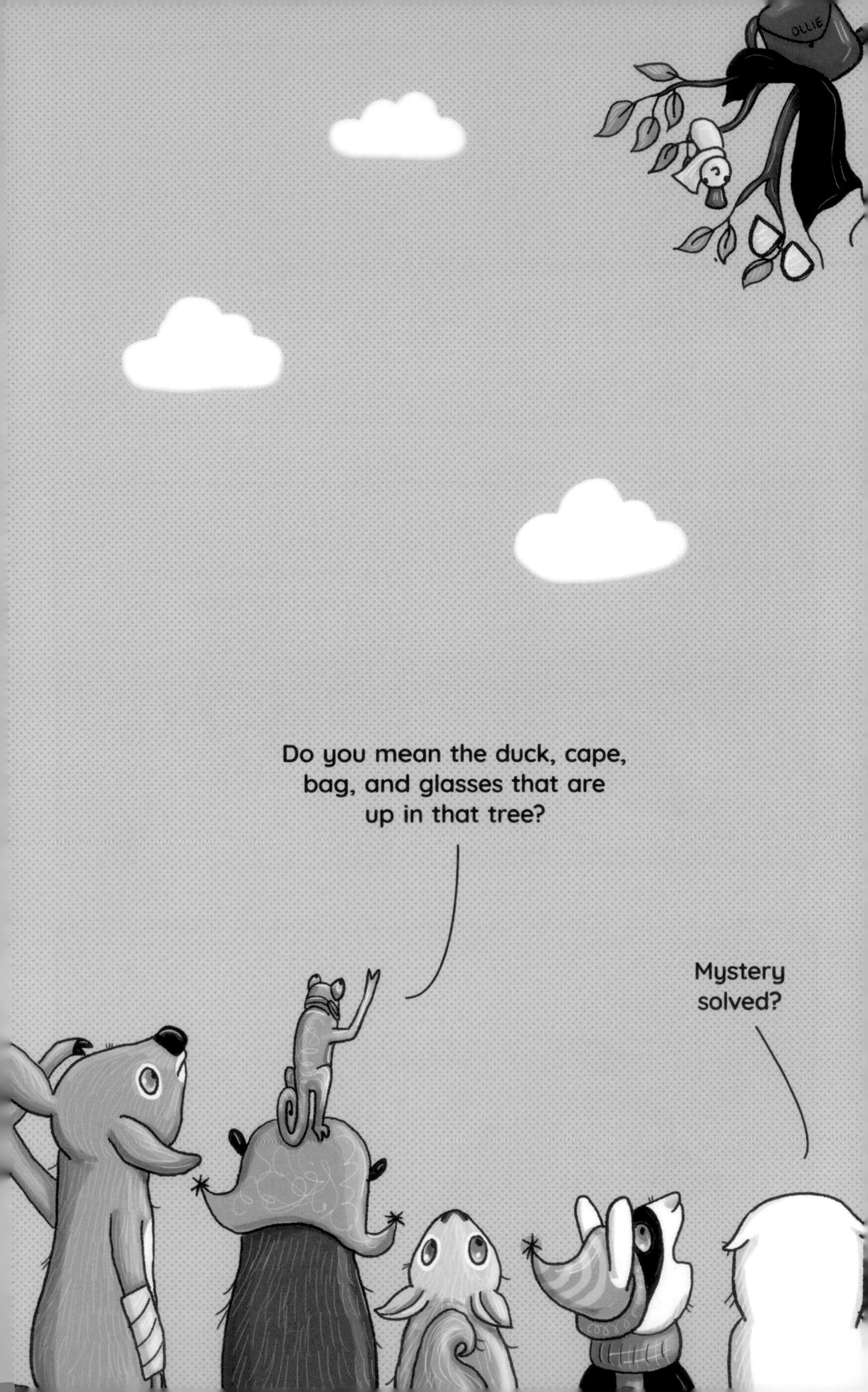
OLLIE
Do you mean the duck, cape, bag, and glasses that are up in that tree?
Mystery solved?

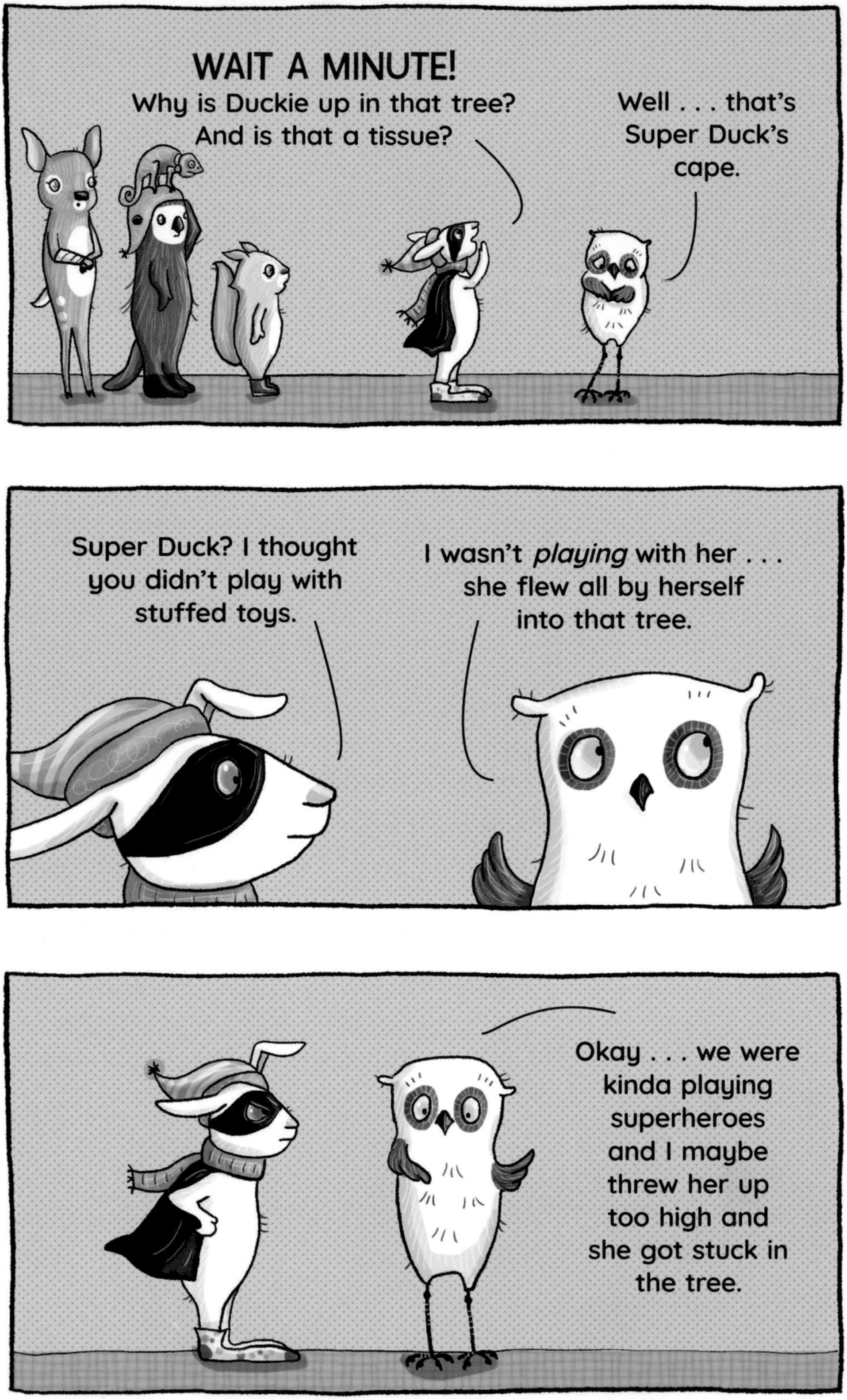
WAIT A MINUTE!
Why is Duckie up in that tree? And is that a tissue?
Well . . . that's Super Duck's cape.
Super Duck? I thought you didn't play with stuffed toys.
I wasn't *playing* with her . . . she flew all by herself into that tree.
Okay . . . we were kinda playing superheroes and I maybe threw her up too high and she got stuck in the tree.

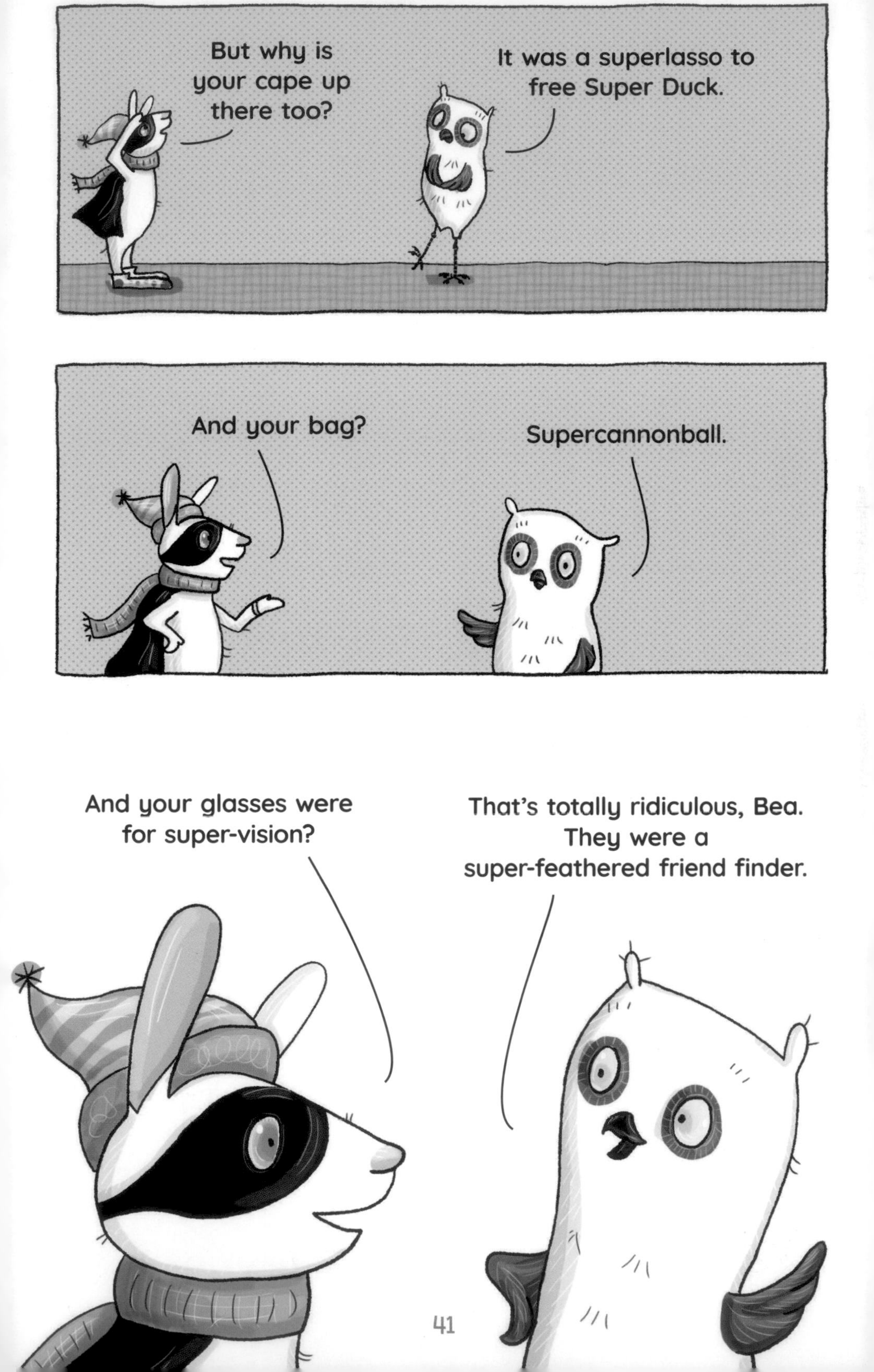
But why is your cape up there too?
It was a superlasso to free Super Duck.
And your bag?
Supercannonball.
And your glasses were for super-vision?
That's totally ridiculous, Bea. They were a super-feathered friend finder.

But none of it
worked.
I'm really
sorry, Bea.

42

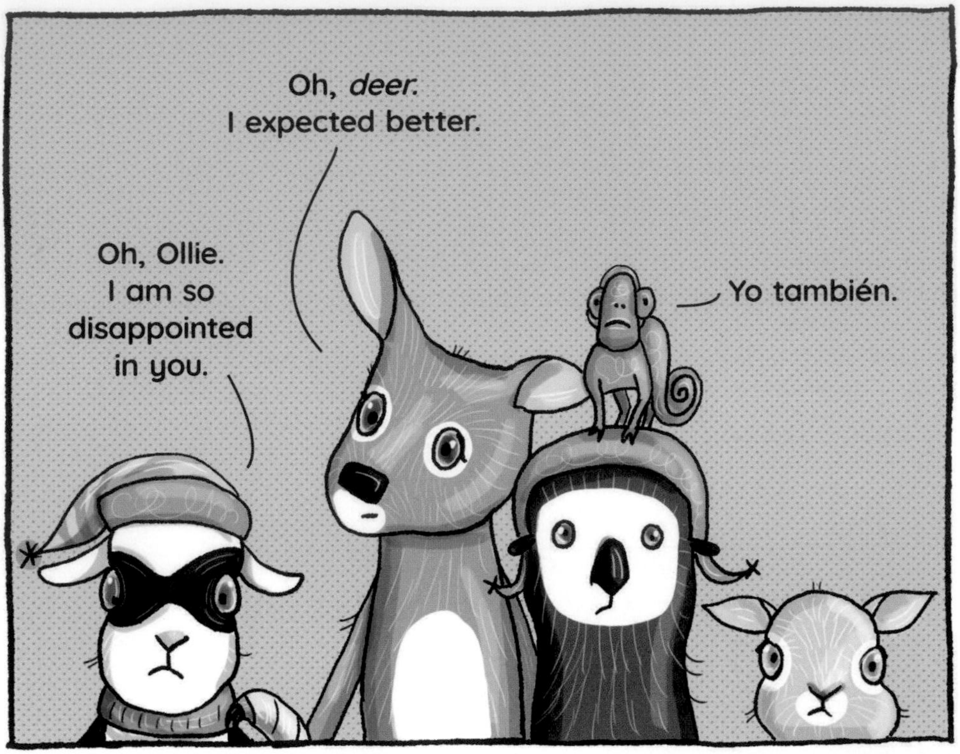
Oh, Ollie.
I am so
disappointed
in you.
Oh, *deer*.
I expected better.
Yo también.

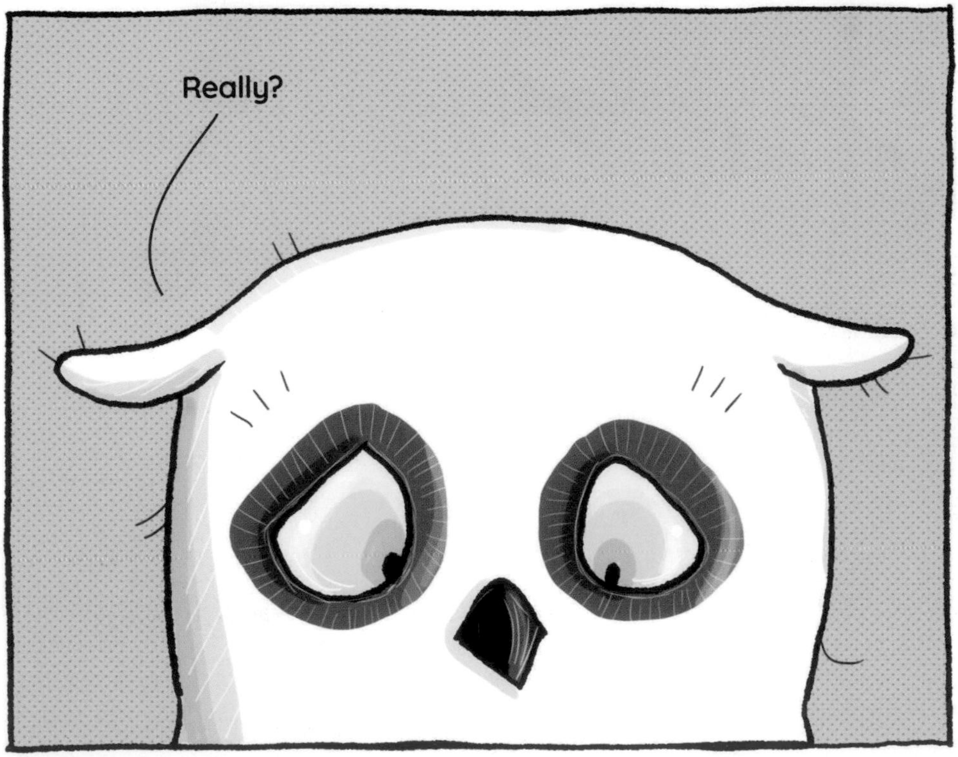
Really?

CHAPTER 5
TREE-MENDOUSLY GREAT

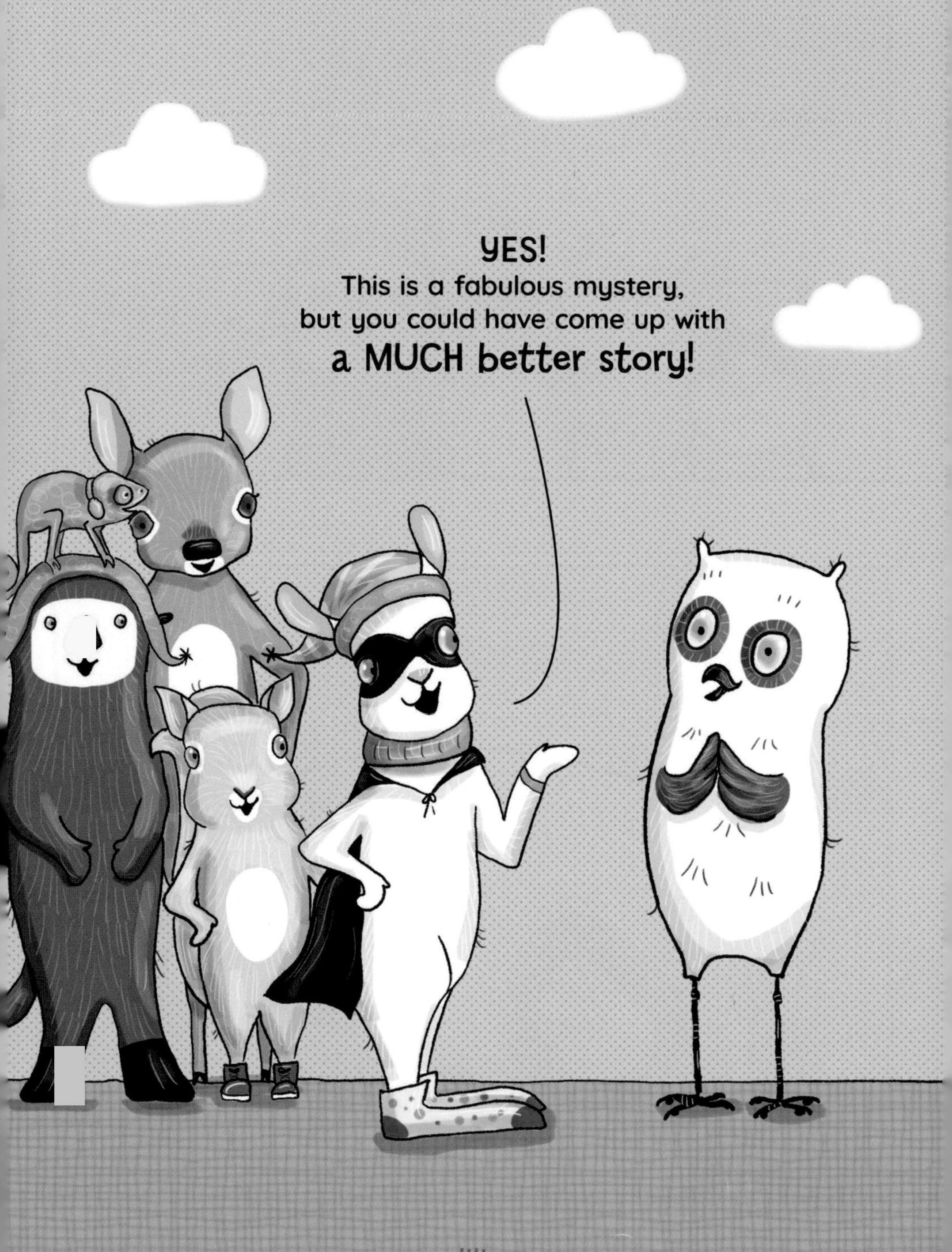
YES!
This is a fabulous mystery,
but you could have come up with
a MUCH better story!

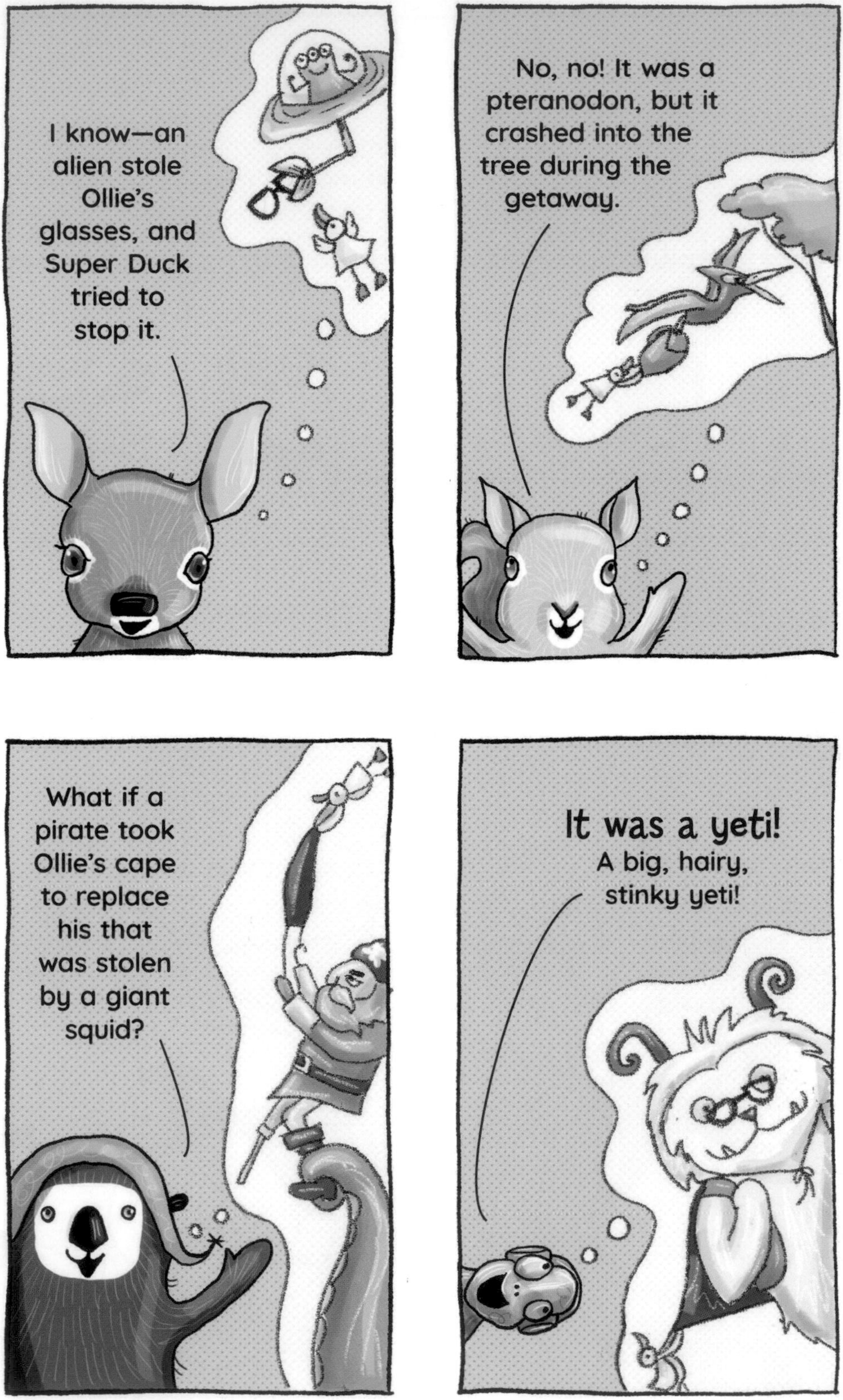
I know—an alien stole Ollie's glasses, and Super Duck tried to stop it.
No, no! It was a pteranodon, but it crashed into the tree during the getaway.
What if a pirate took Ollie's cape to replace his that was stolen by a giant squid?
It was a yeti!
A big, hairy, stinky yeti!

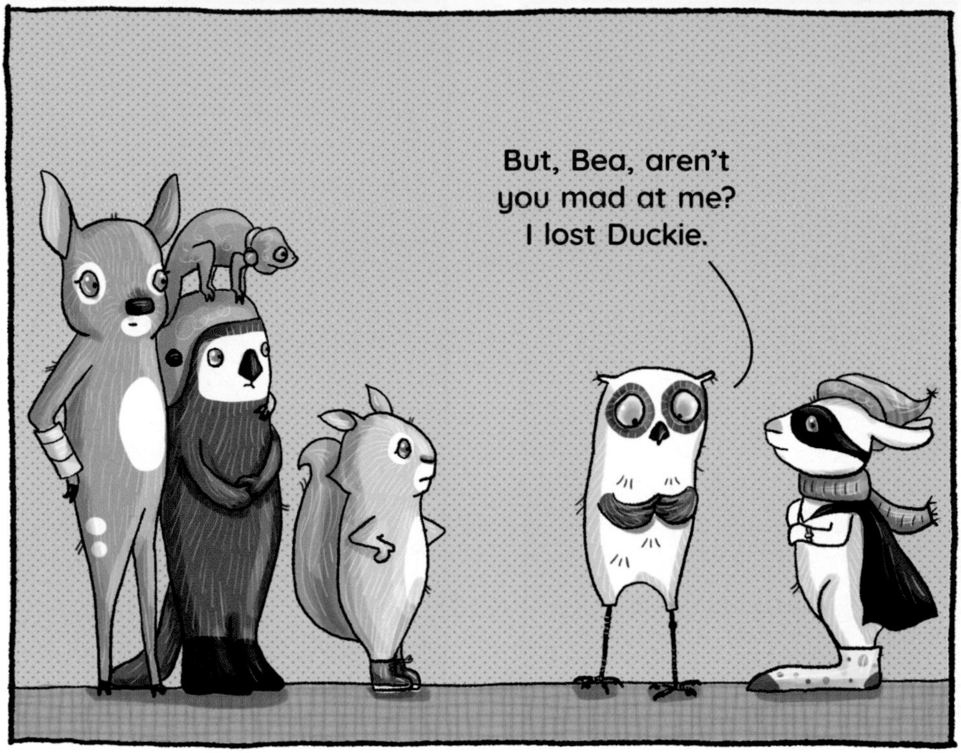
But, Bea, aren't you mad at me? I lost Duckie.

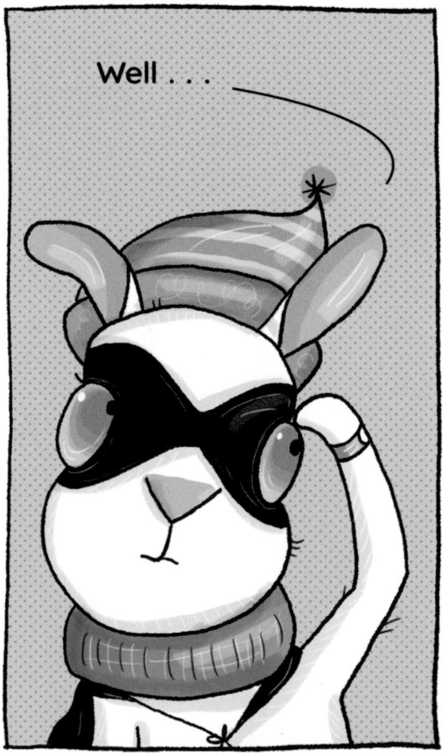
Well . . .

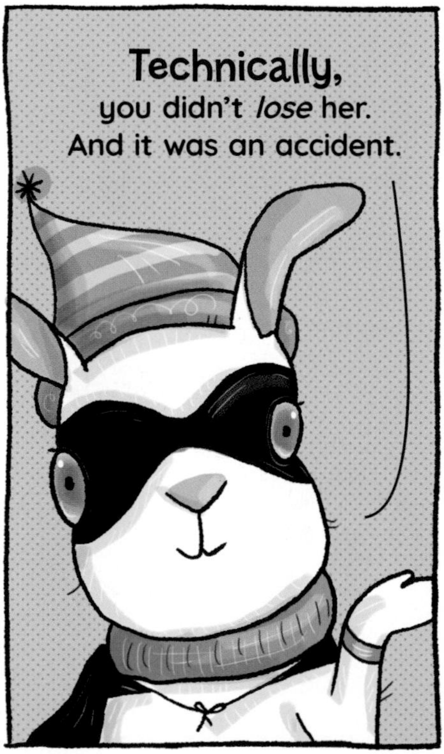
Technically,
you didn't *lose* her. And it was an accident.

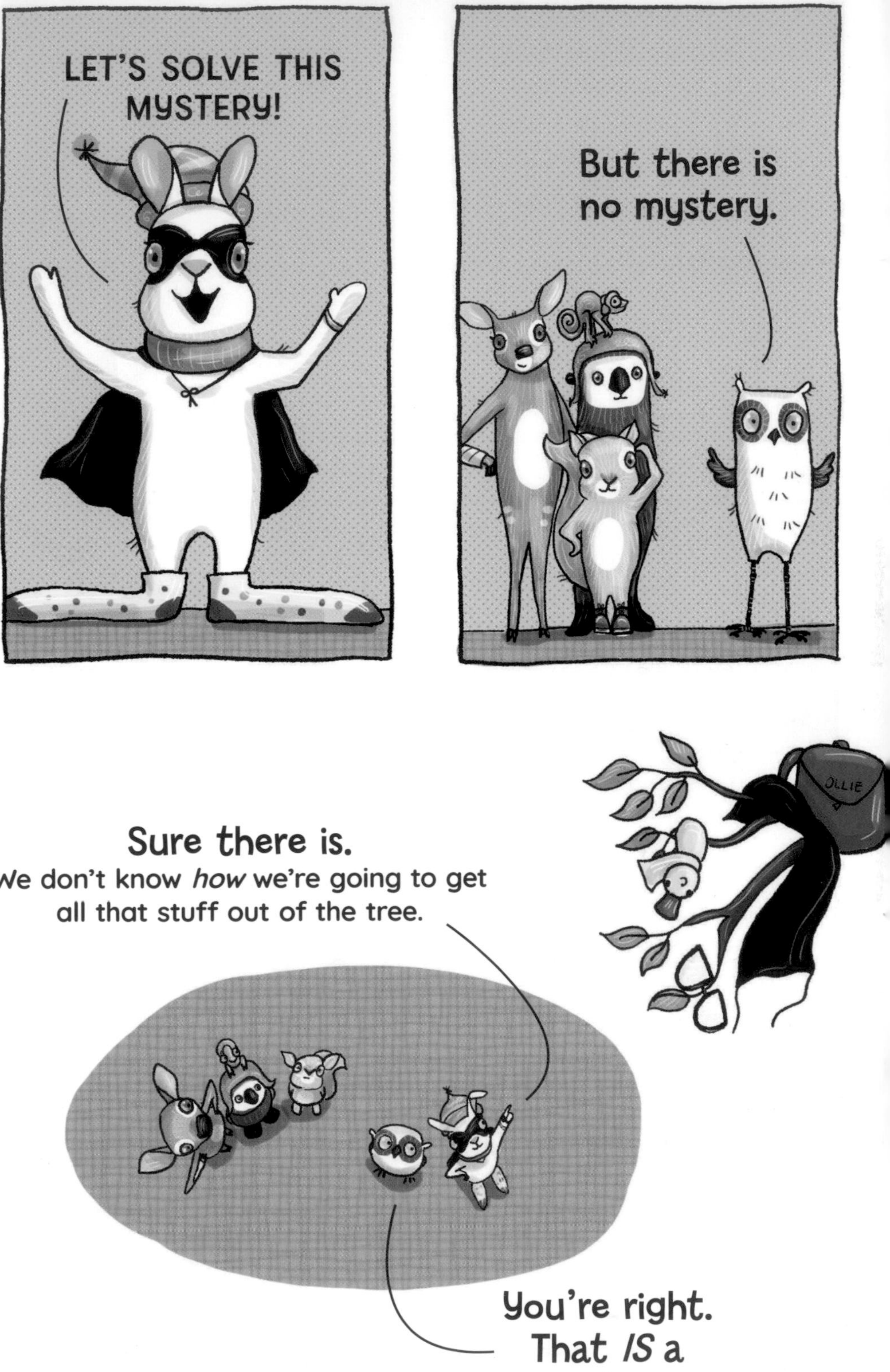
LET'S SOLVE THIS MYSTERY!
But there is no mystery.
OLLIE
Sure there is.
We don't know *how* we're going to get all that stuff out of the tree.
You're right. That *IS* a mystery.

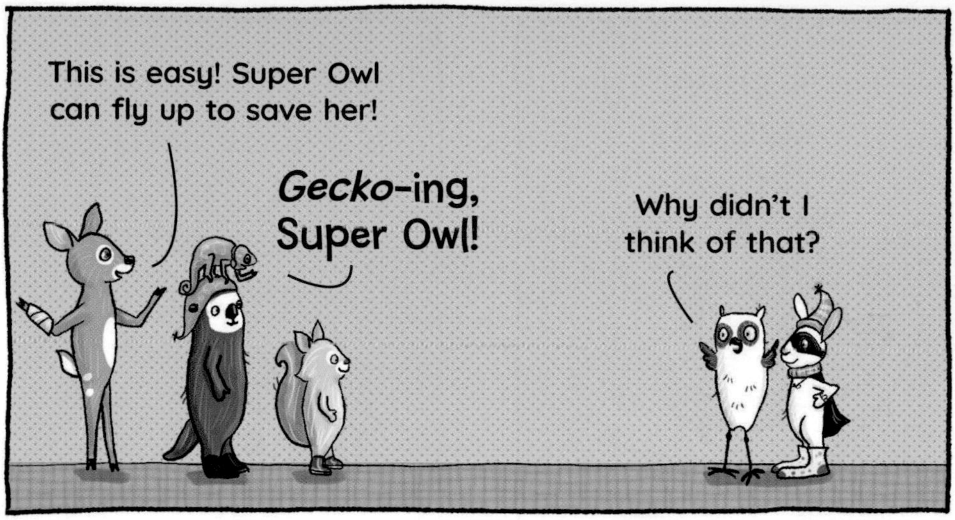
This is easy! Super Owl can fly up to save her!
Gecko-ing, Super Owl!
Why didn't I think of that?

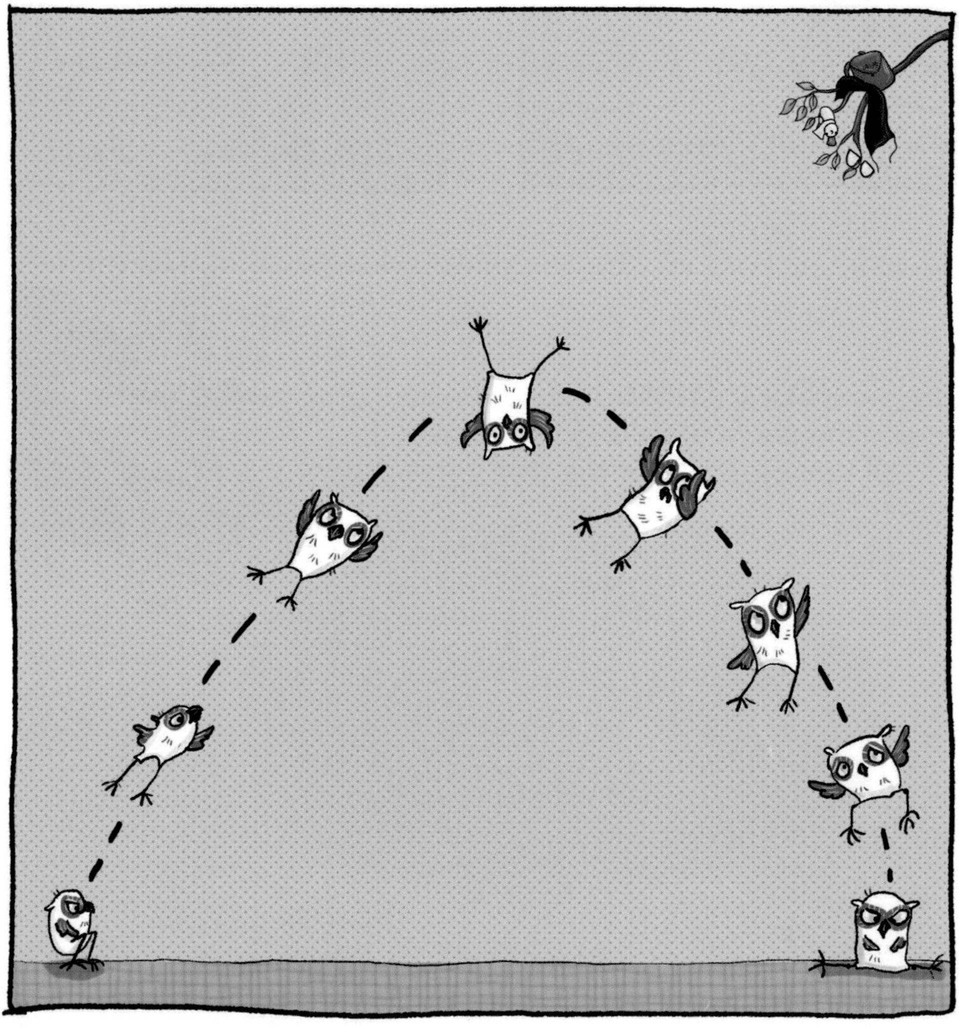

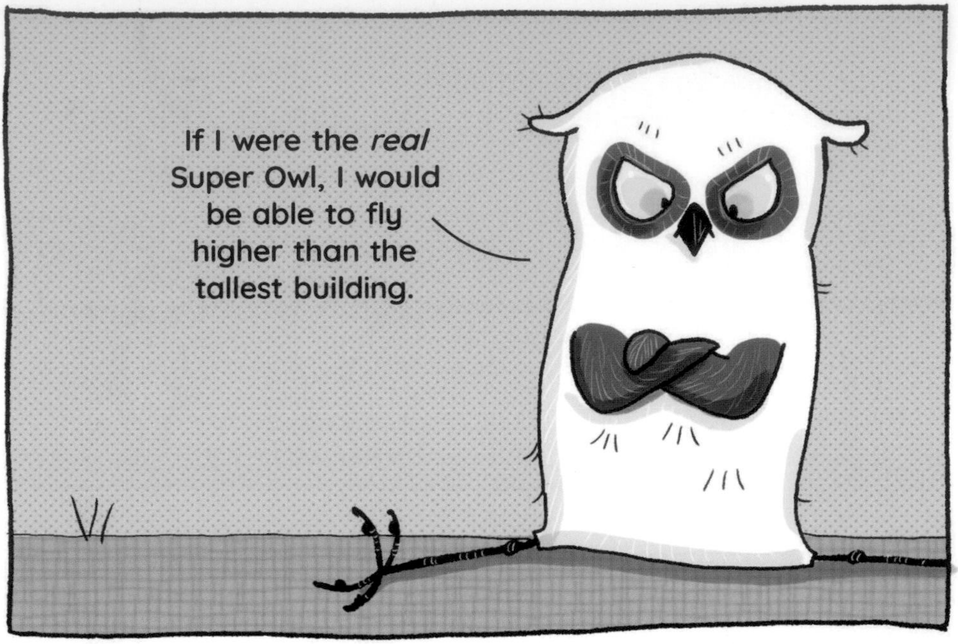
If I were the *real* Super Owl, I would be able to fly higher than the tallest building.

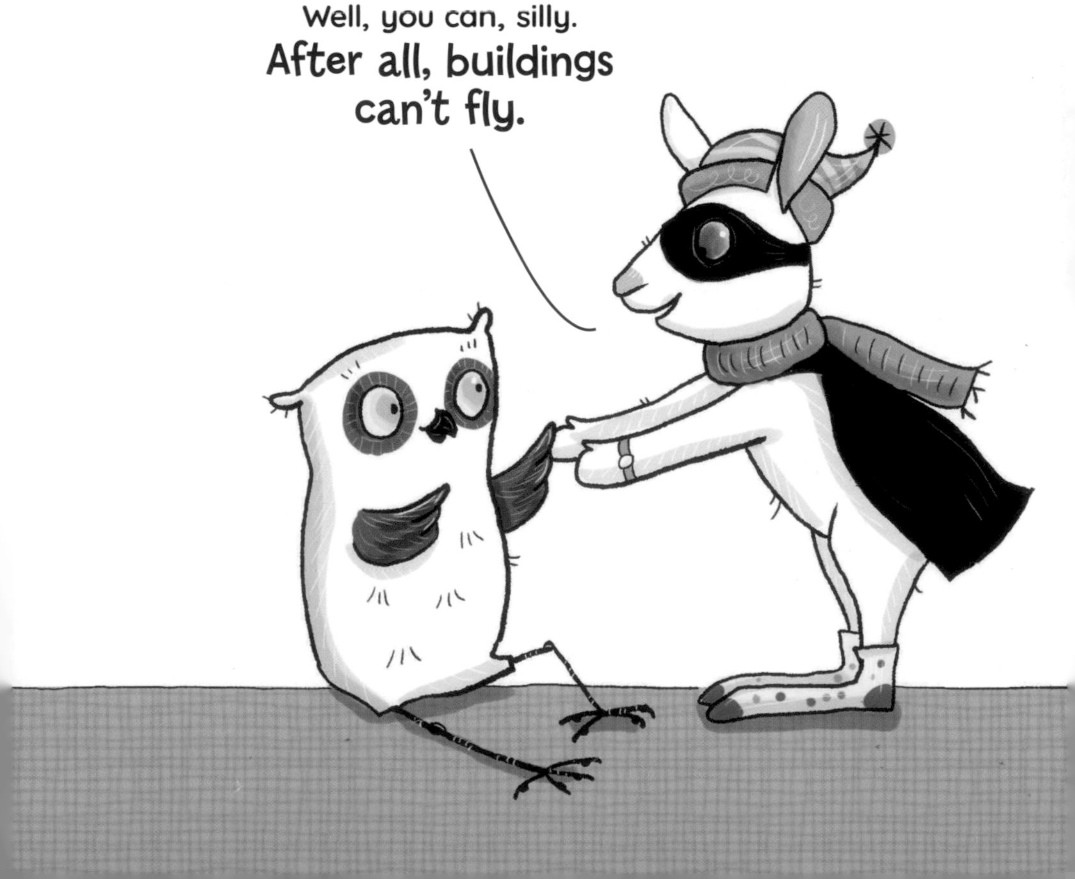
Well, you can, silly.
After all, buildings can't fly.

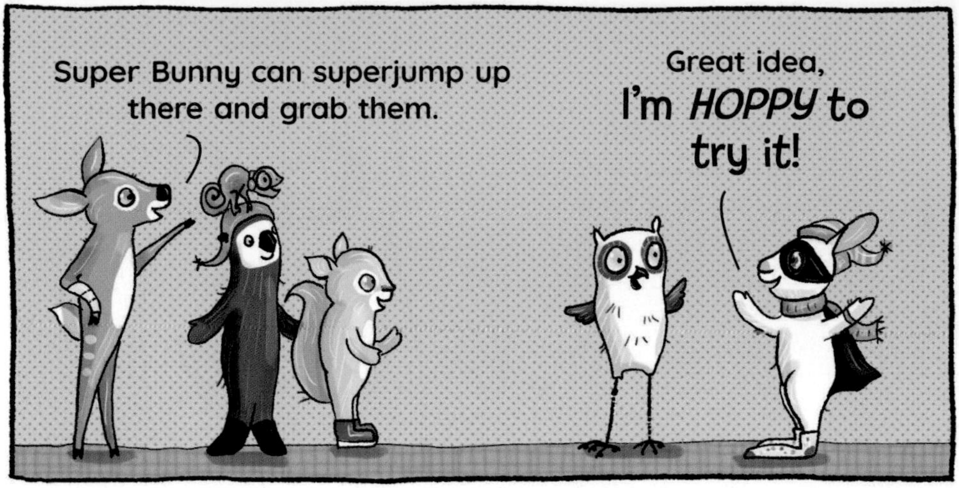
Super Bunny can superjump up there and grab them.
Great idea, I'm *HOPPY* to try it!

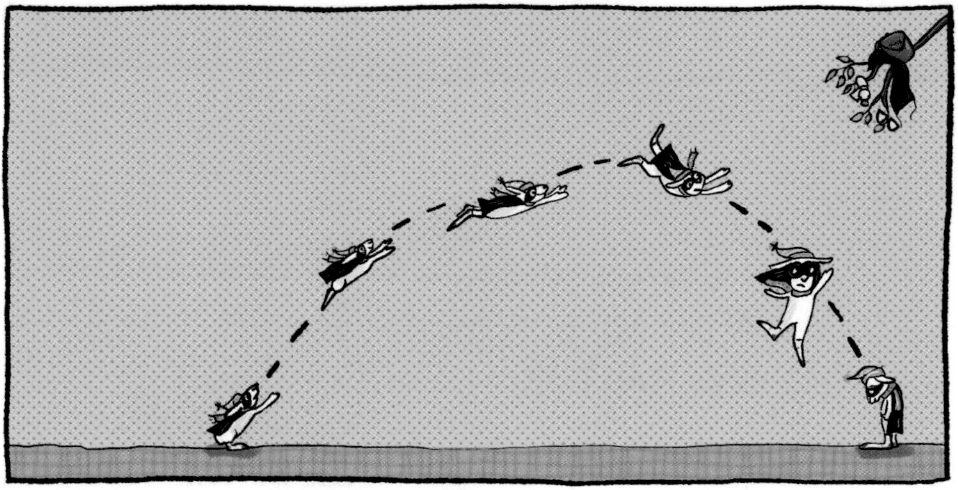

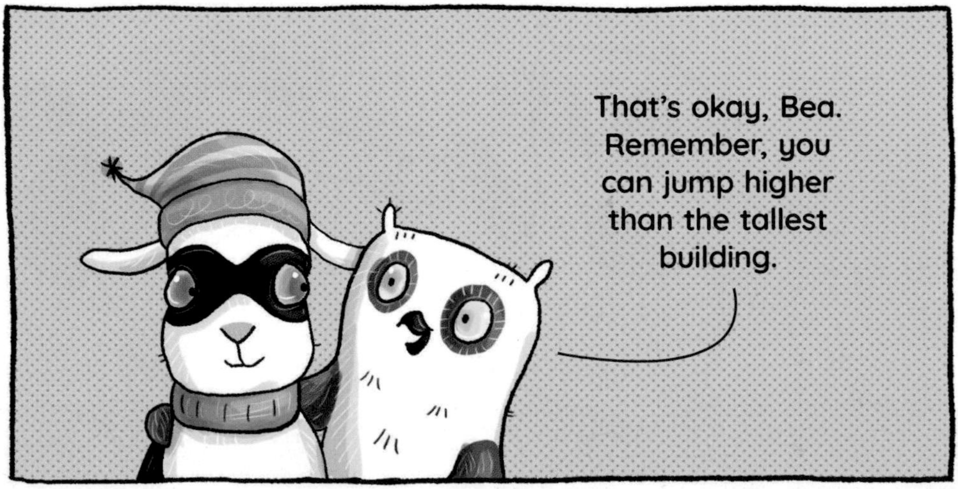
That's okay, Bea. Remember, you can jump higher than the tallest building.

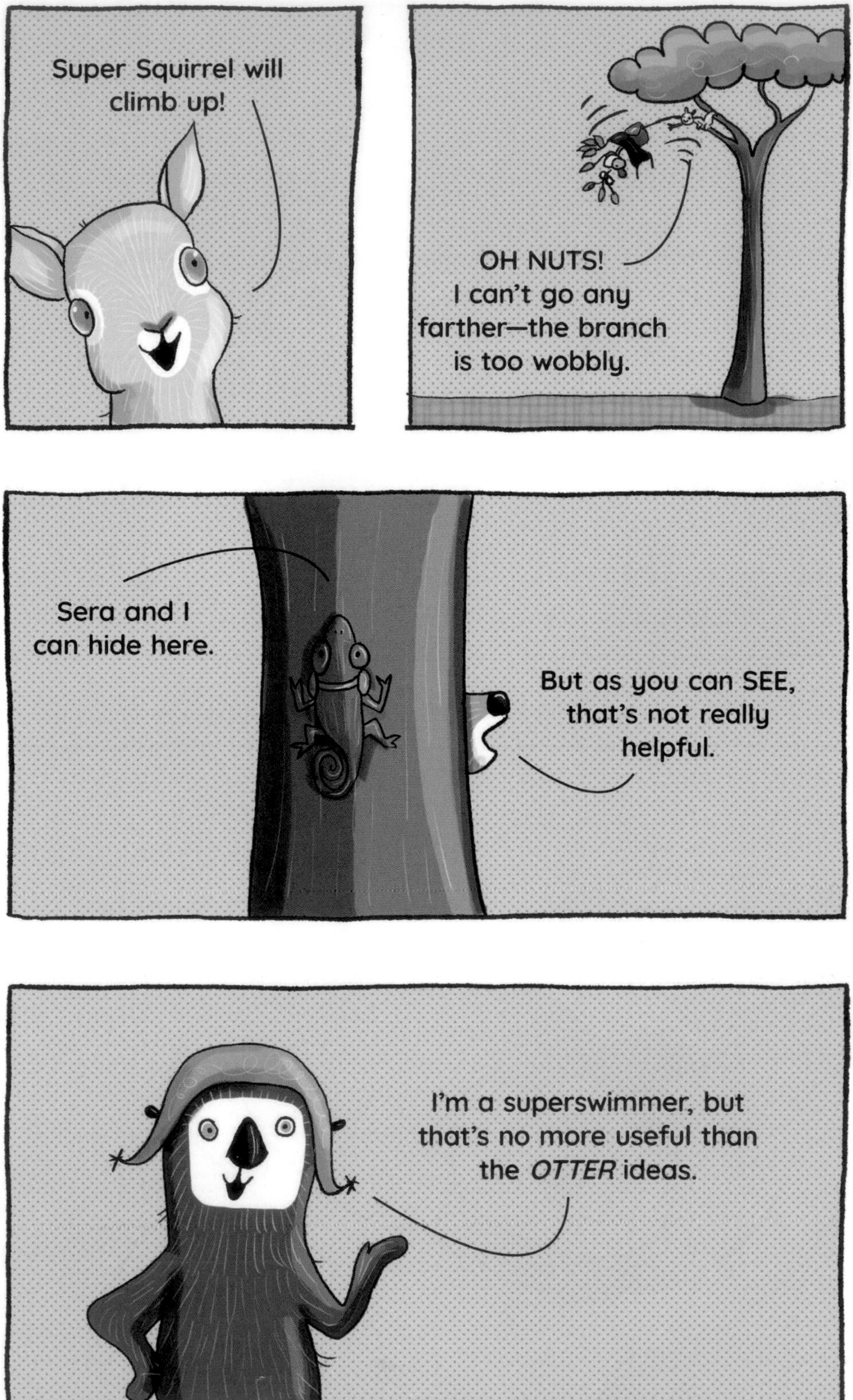
Super Squirrel will climb up!
OH NUTS! I can't go any farther—the branch is too wobbly.
Sera and I can hide here.
But as you can SEE, that's not really helpful.
I'm a superswimmer, but that's no more useful than the *OTTER* ideas.

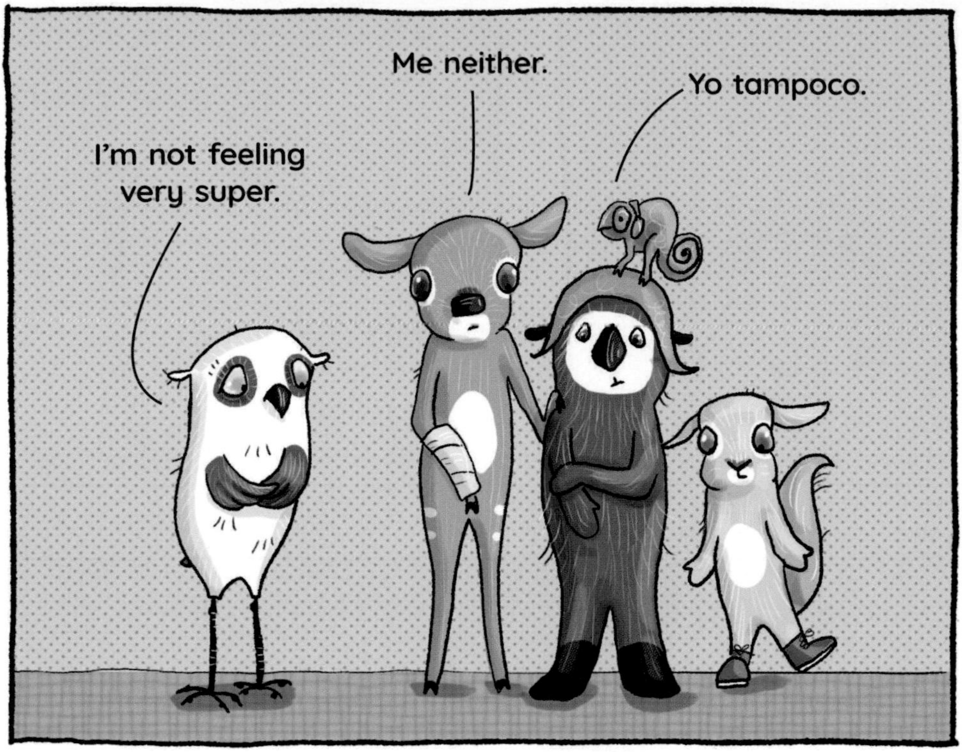
I'm not feeling very super.
Me neither.
Yo tampoco.

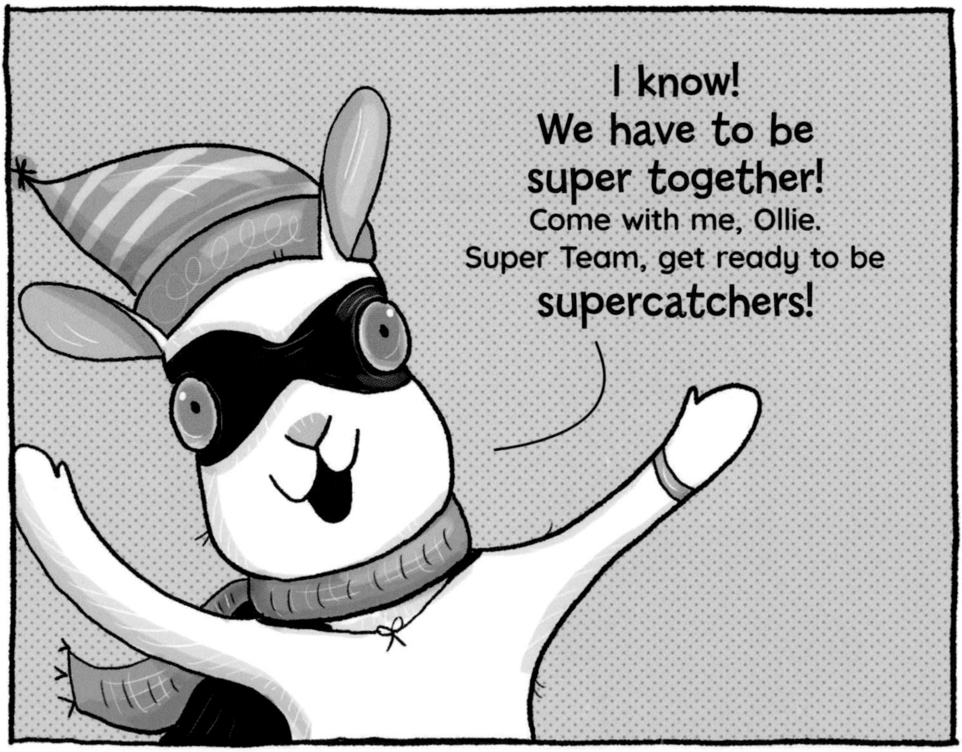
I know!
We have to be super together!
Come with me, Ollie.
Super Team, get ready to be supercatchers!

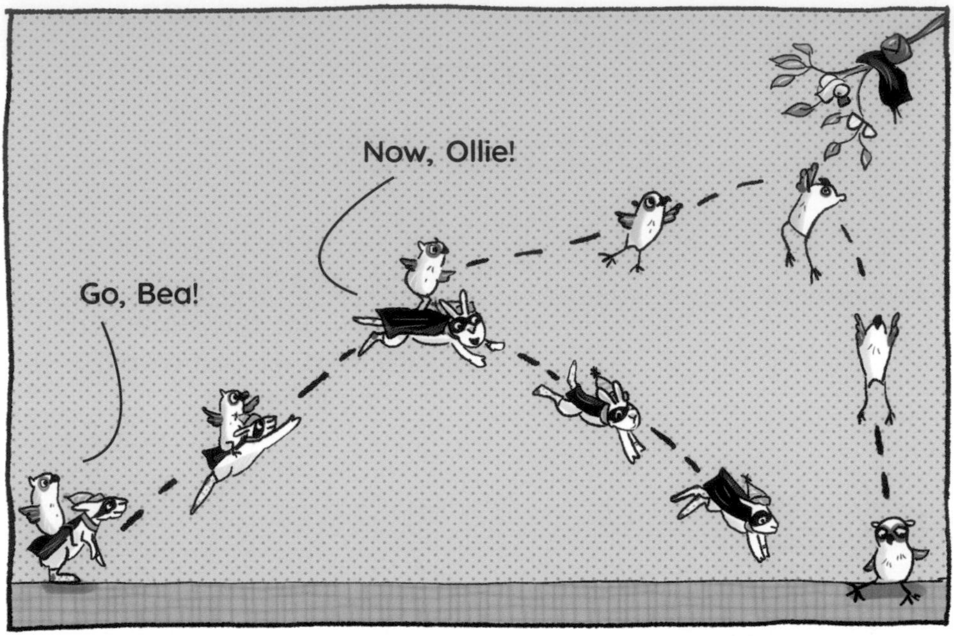
Go, Bea!
Now, Ollie!

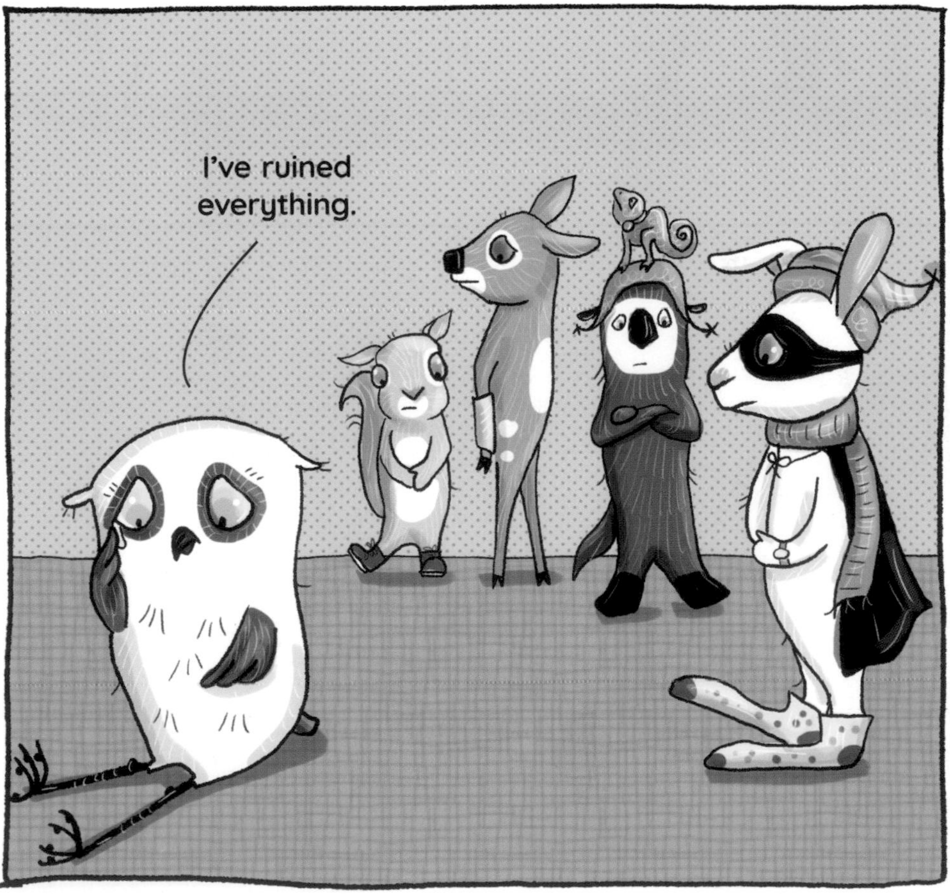
I've ruined everything.

CHAPTER 6
LUCKY DUCKIE

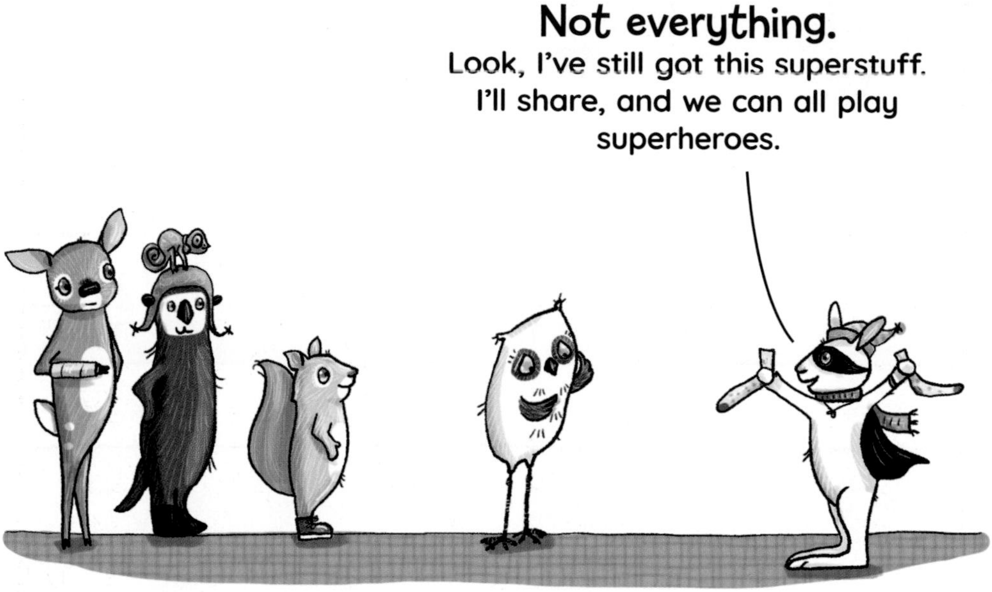
Not everything.
Look, I've still got this superstuff. I'll share, and we can all play superheroes.

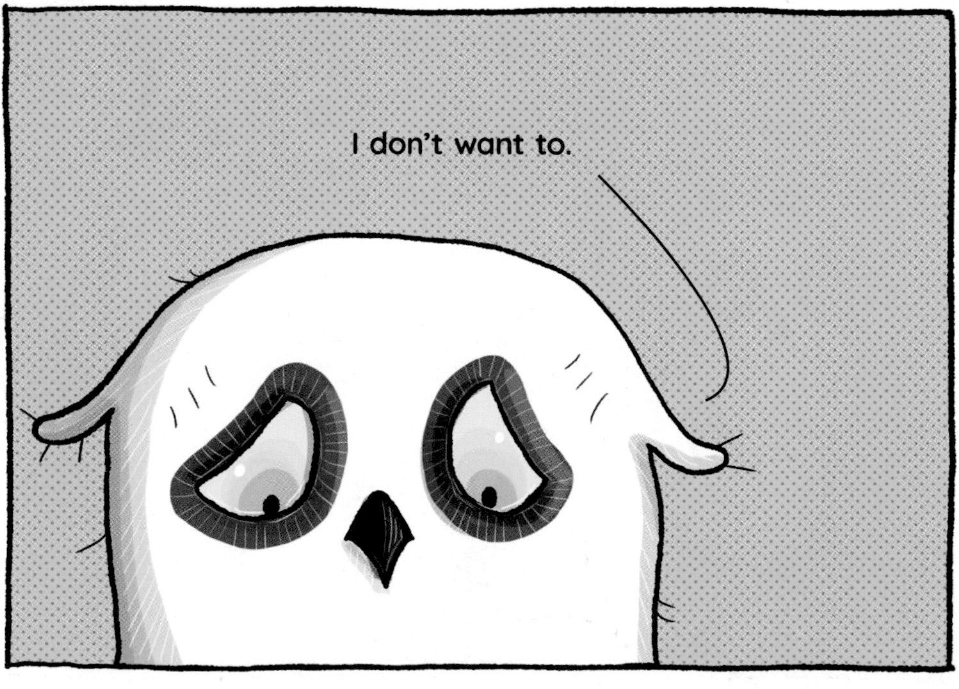
I don't want to.

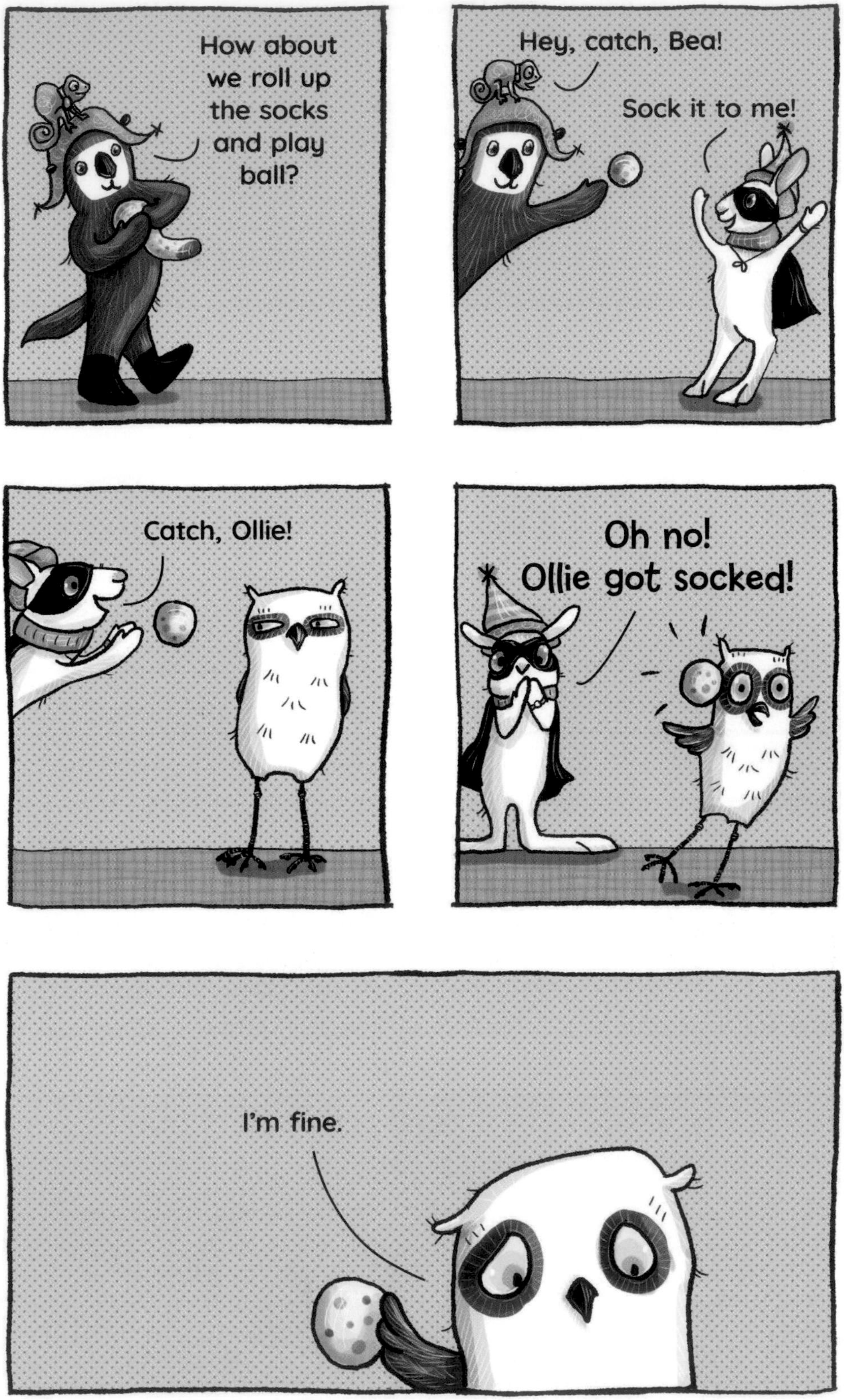
How about we roll up the socks and play ball?
Hey, catch, Bea!
Sock it to me!
Catch, Ollie!
Oh no! Ollie got socked!
I'm fine.

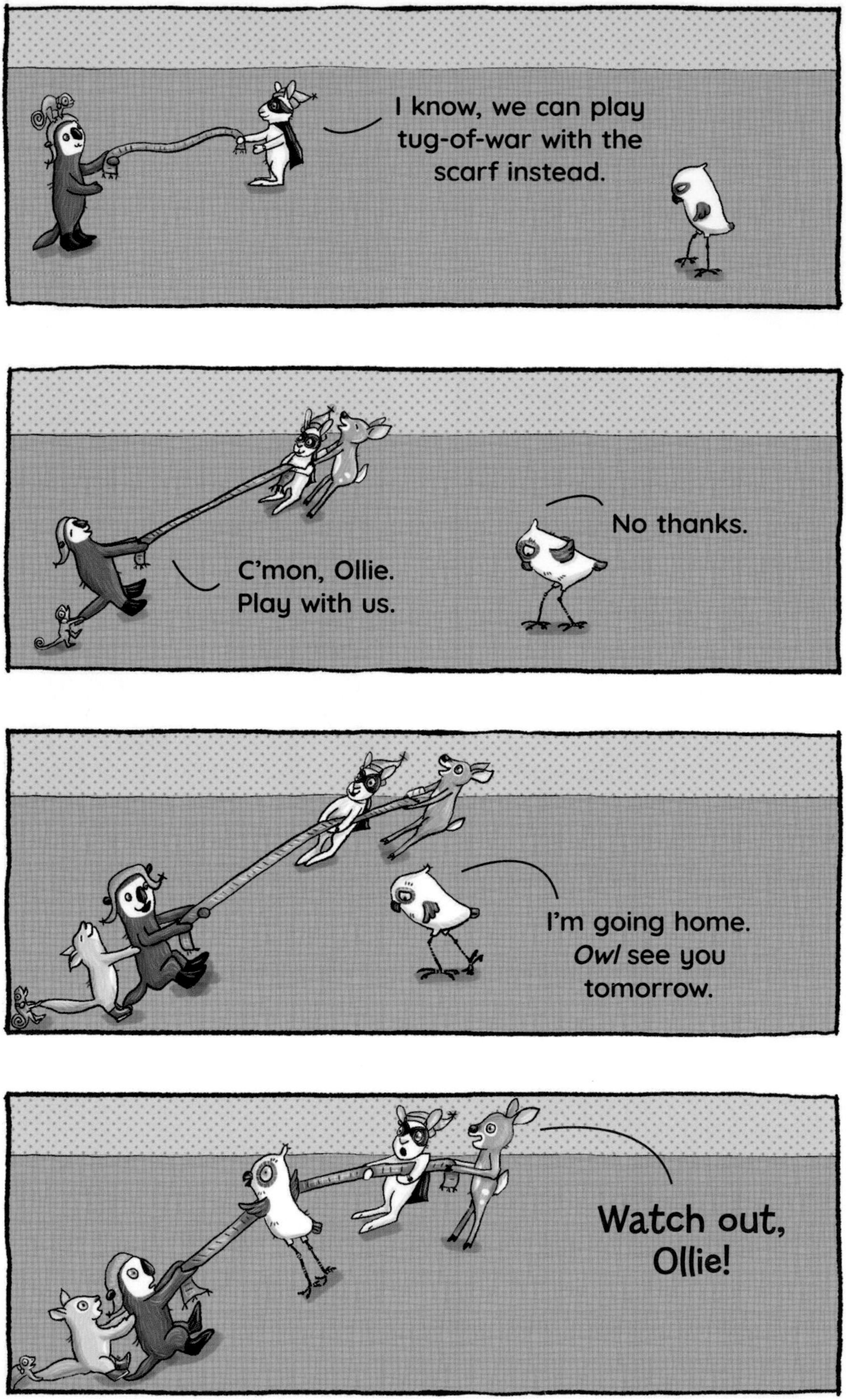
I know, we can play tug-of-war with the scarf instead.
C'mon, Ollie. Play with us.
No thanks.
I'm going home. *Owl* see you tomorrow.
Watch out, Ollie!

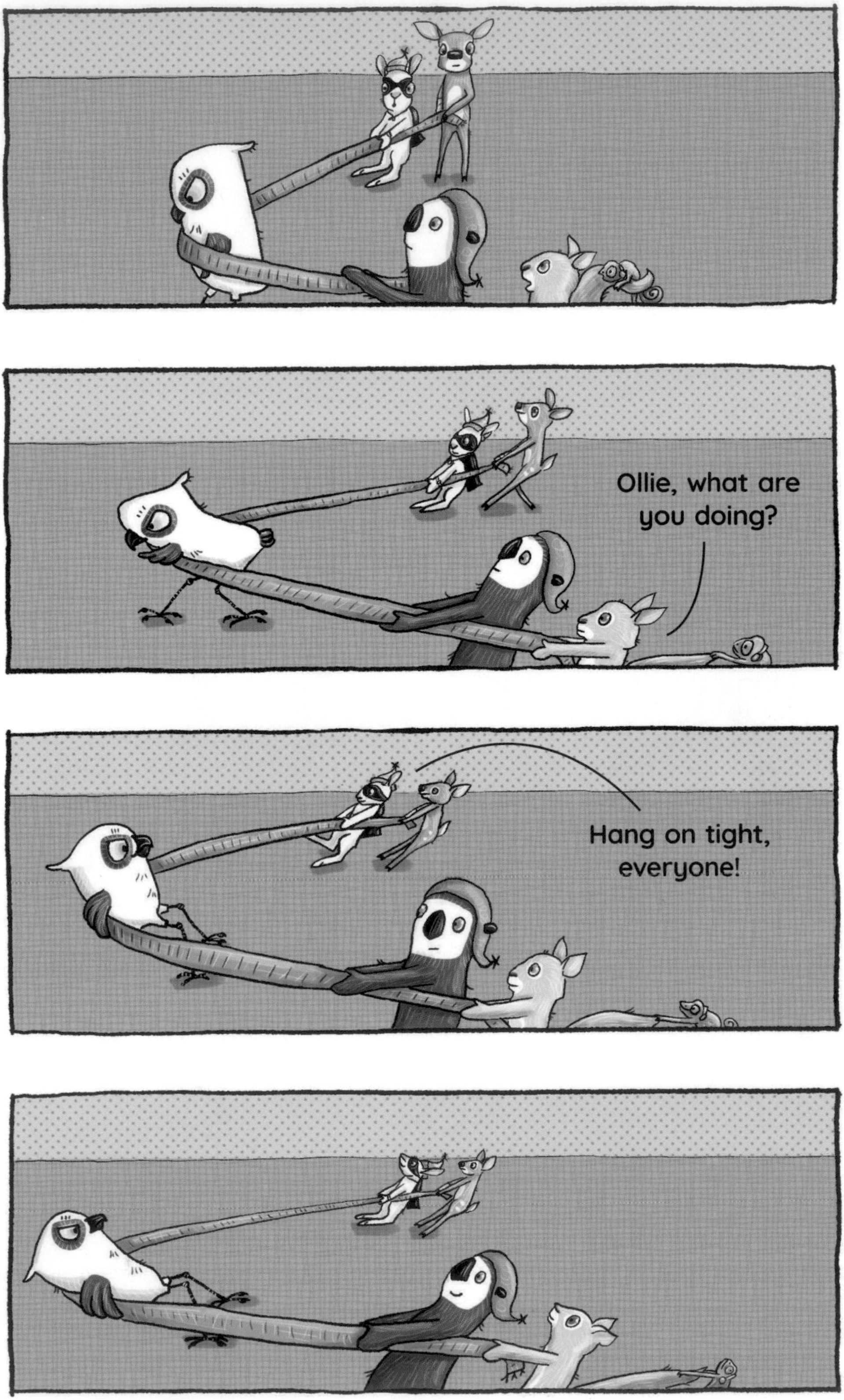
Ollie, what are you doing?
Hang on tight, everyone!

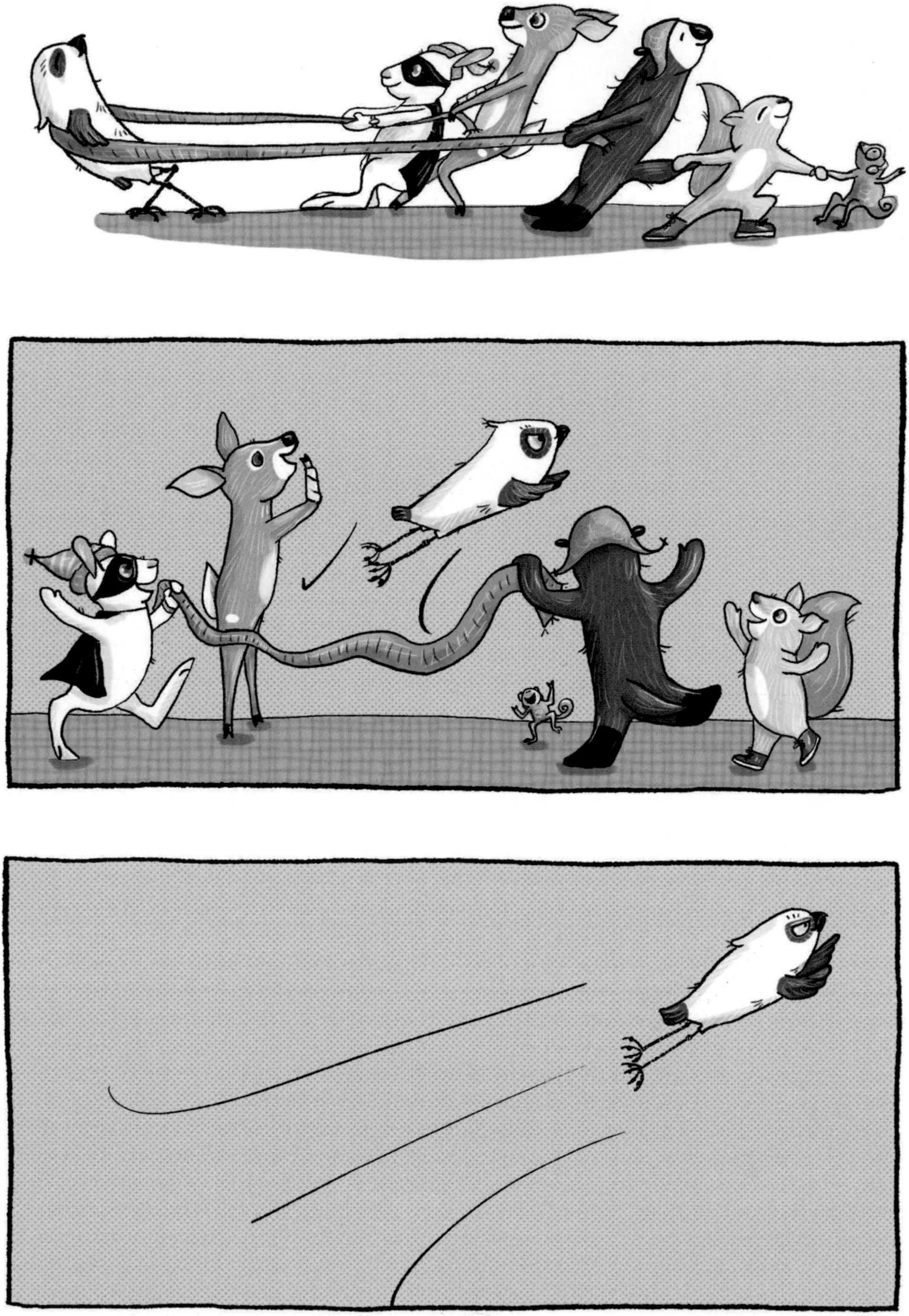

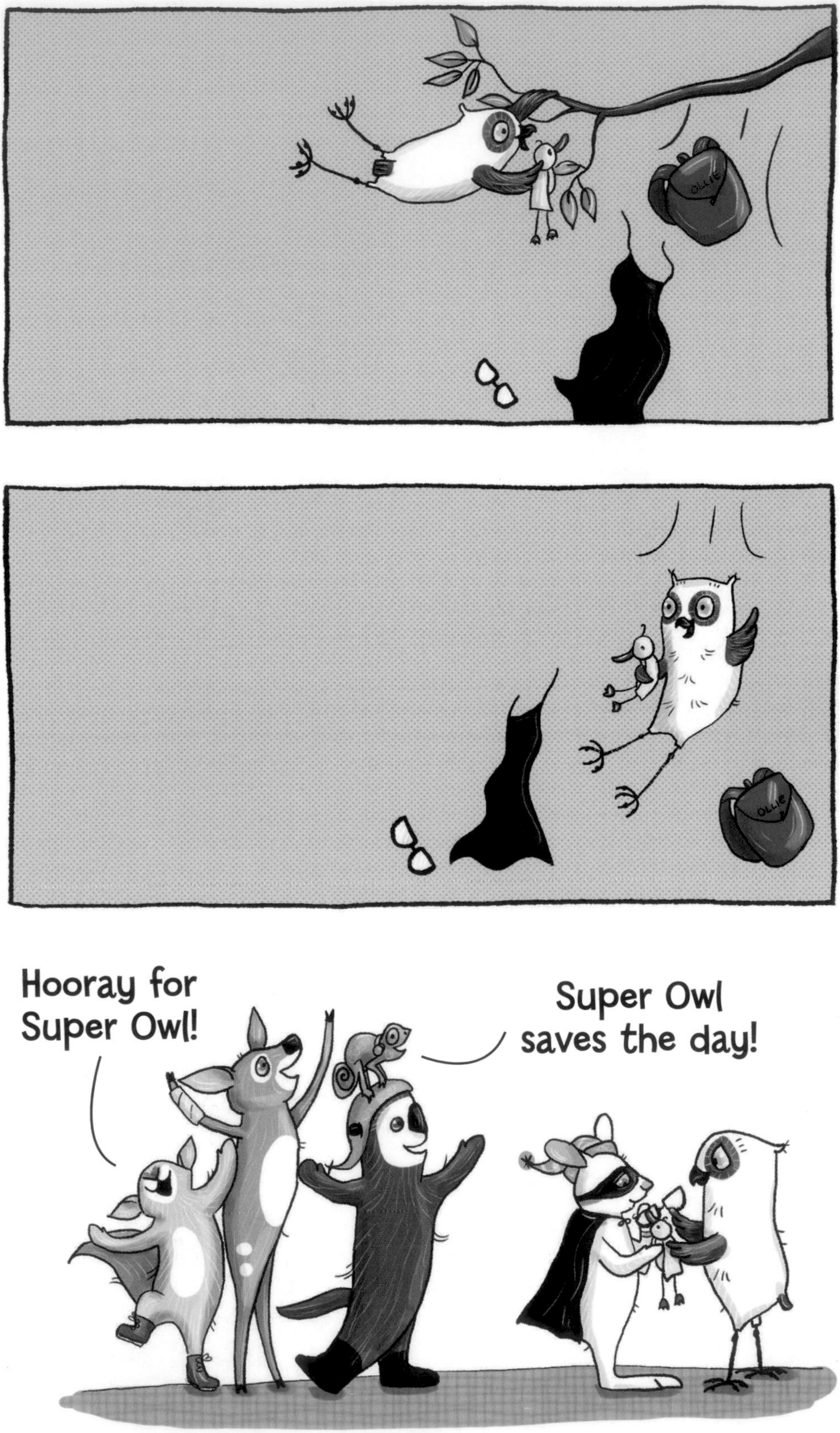
OLLIE
OLLIE
Hooray for Super Owl!
Super Owl saves the day!

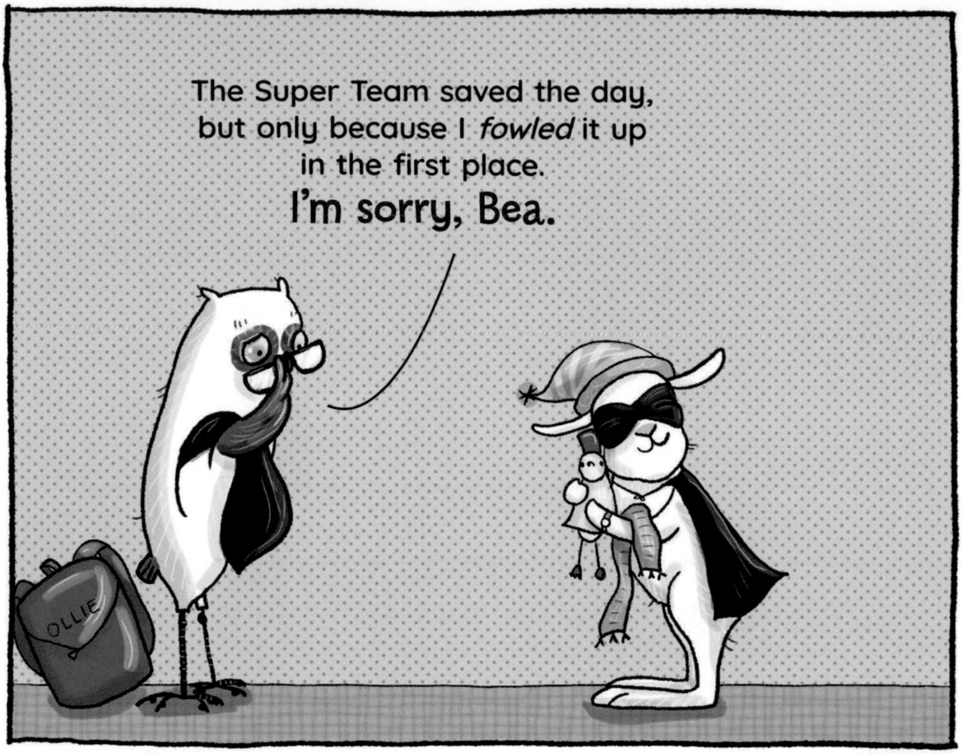
The Super Team saved the day, but only because I *fowled* it up in the first place.
I'm sorry, Bea.
OLLIE

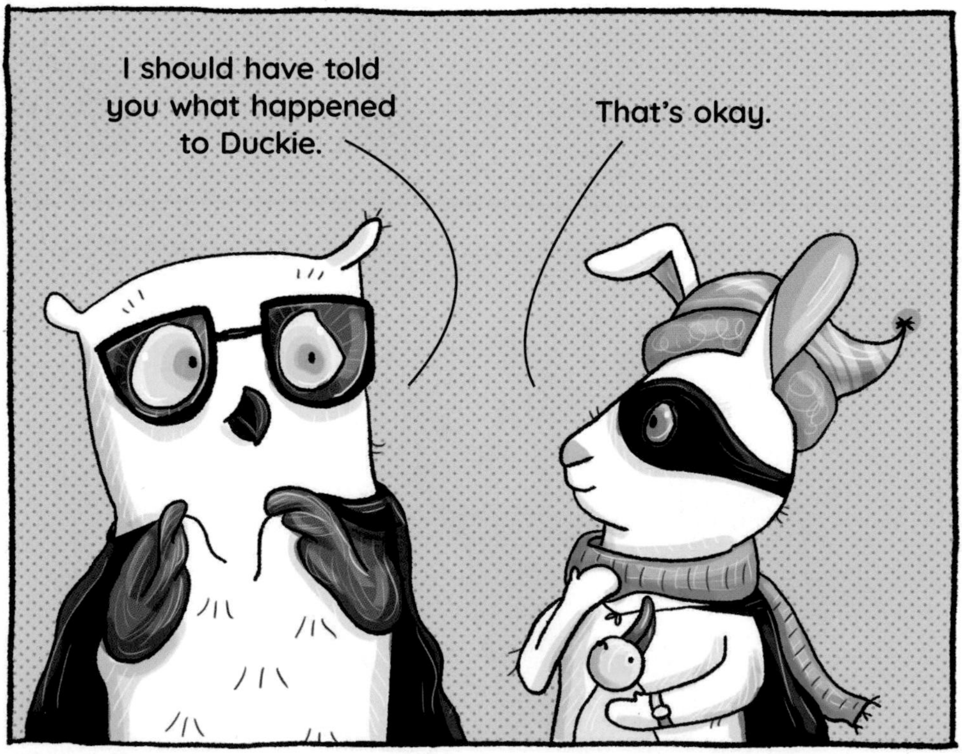
I should have told you what happened to Duckie.
That's okay.

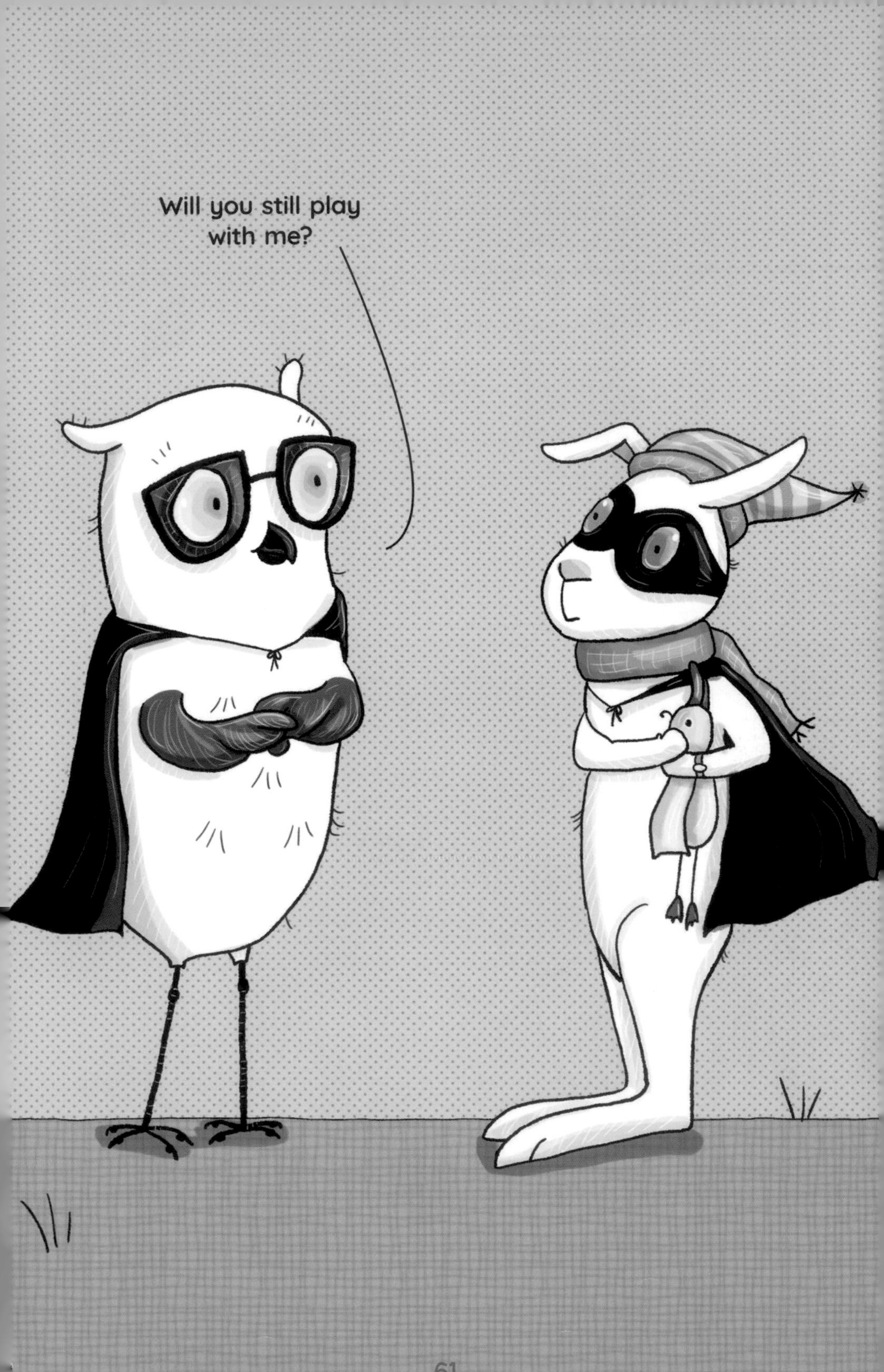
Will you still play with me?

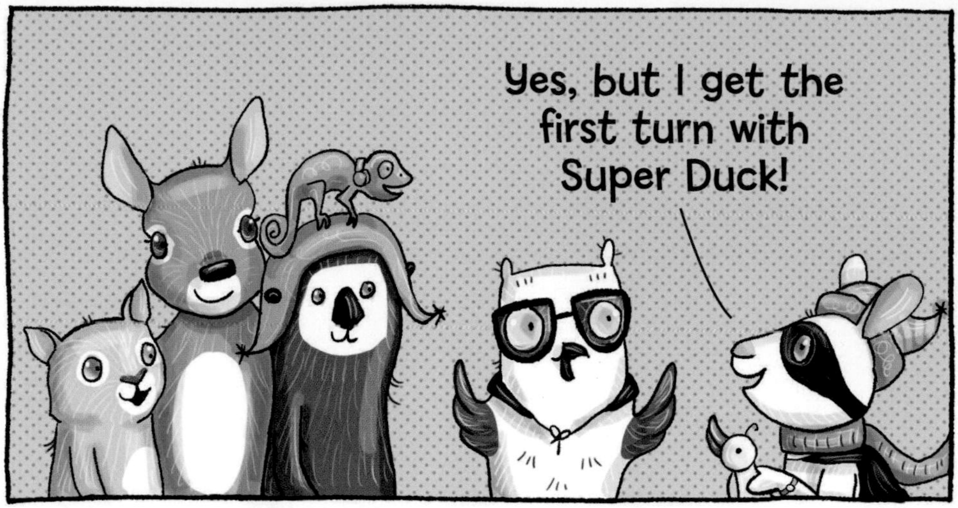
Yes, but I get the first turn with Super Duck!

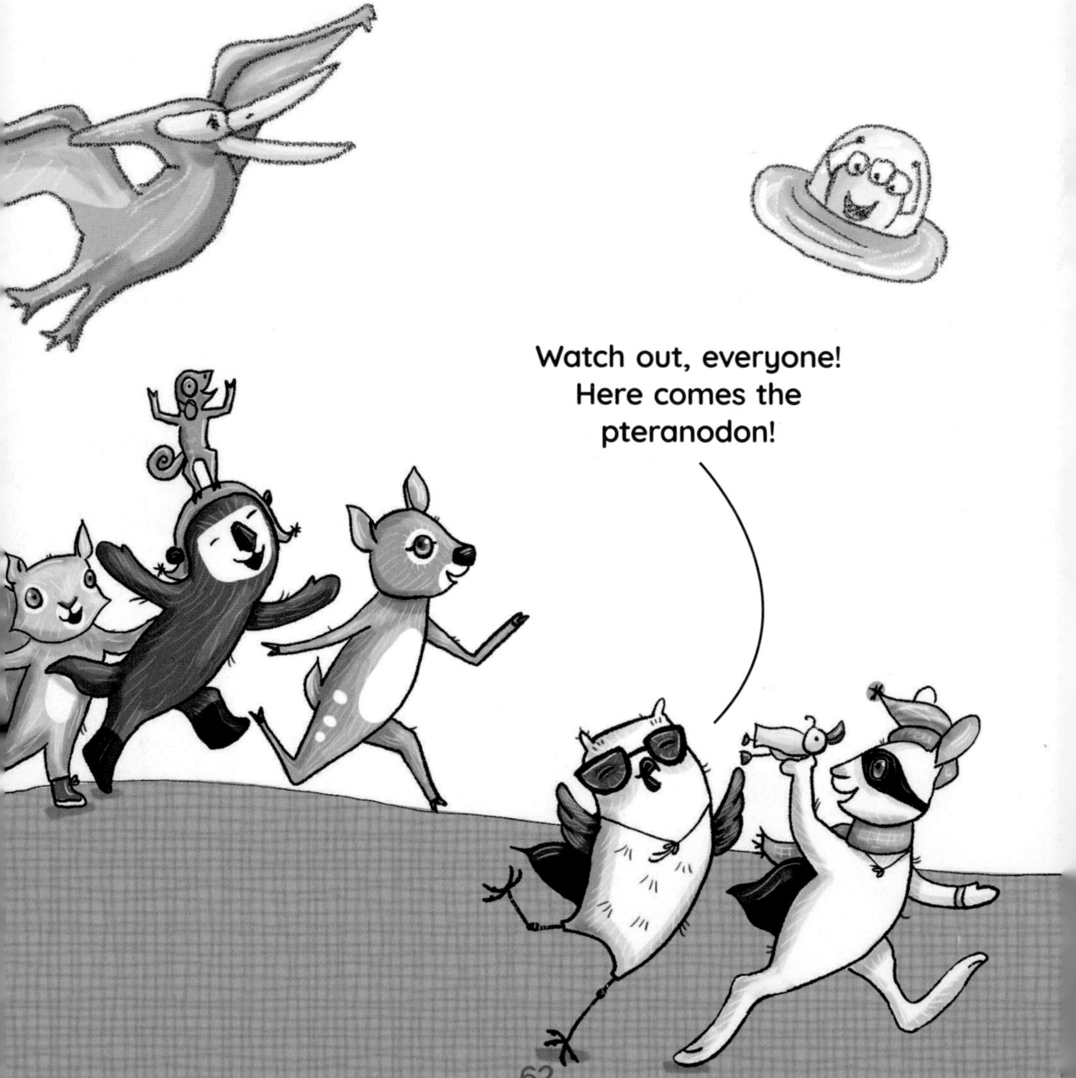
Watch out, everyone! Here comes the pteranodon!

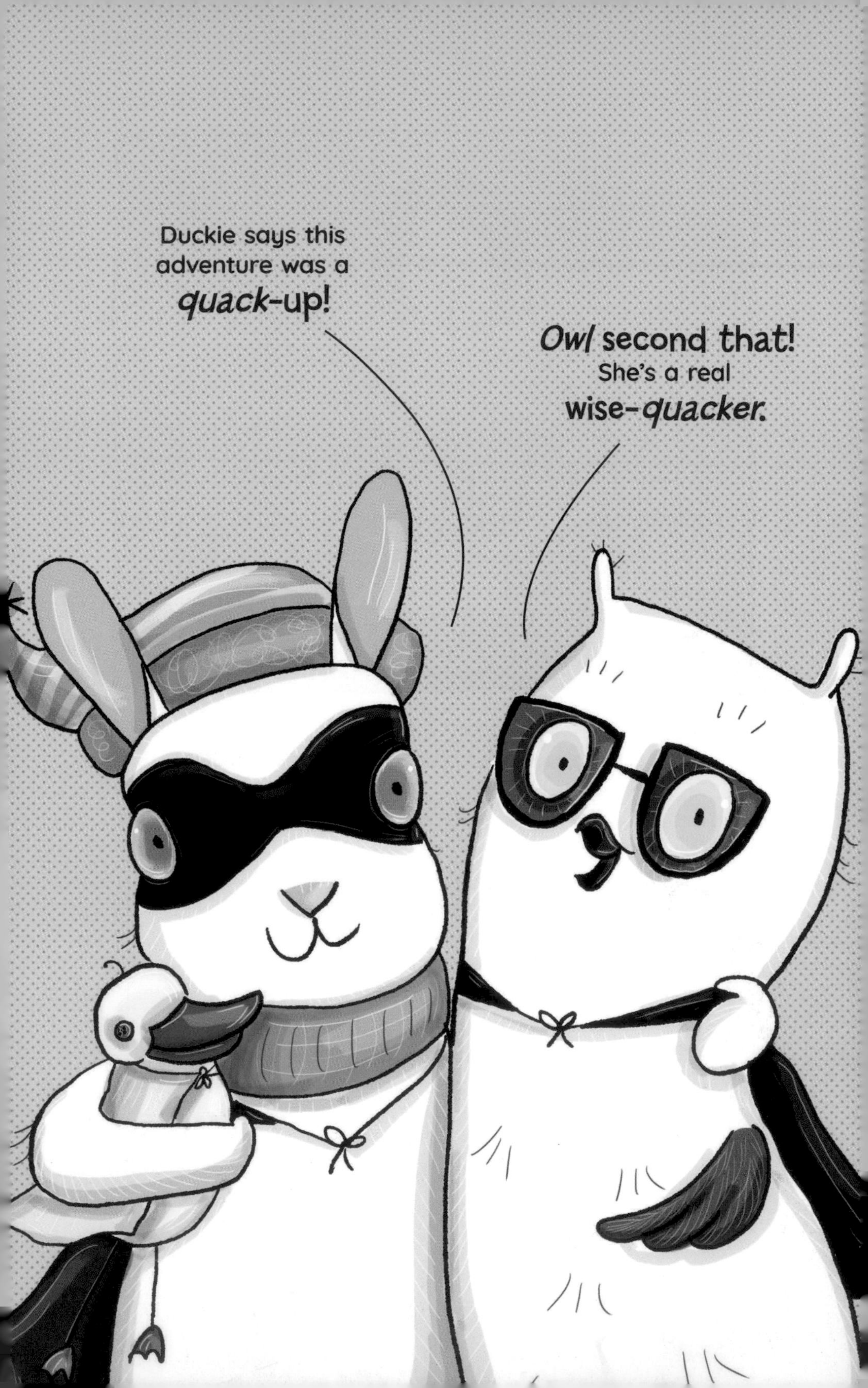
Duckie says this adventure was a *quack*-up!
Owl second that! She's a real wise-*quacker*.

ABOUT THE CREATOR

Renée Treml was born and raised in the
United States and now lives on the beautiful Surf
Coast in Australia. Her stories and illustrations
are inspired by nature and influenced by her
background in environmental science. When
Renée is not writing or illustrating, she can be
found walking in the bush or on the beach, or
exploring museums, zoos, and aquariums with
her family and superenthusiastic little dog.